DÉJÀ VU McGREW AND HIS TANK CREW

By
C. A. Powell

Copyright © 2021 C. A. Powell
All rights reserved.

Typeset by Amnet Systems

Citation…
The song sung by the Troopers in this story is 'Polly Wolly Doodle' from a film titled The Littlest Rebel. *It is a 1935 American drama film directed by David Butler and starring Shirley Temple.*

Thanks to…
All the wonderful facebook.com/AuthorC.A.Powell page of friends who offered information about my many questions concerning tanks.

My brother-in-law, Ian. He made a great model of a Cromwell tank. This gave me a great feel to the way Molly (The Tank) would look.

CONTENTS

Chapter 1	A Picture of Wonderful Camaraderie and Delight (North Africa, 1941)	1
Chapter 2	The Burnt-Out Sturmgeschütz (Dutch–German Border – 1945)	19
Chapter 3	Suspicion and Clichés	50
Chapter 4	The Scouting Patrol Get Ready	77
Chapter 5	A Canter Across the Stream	99
Chapter 6	Molly the Most Resplendent Mount	122
Chapter 7	Some More Unwelcome News	138
Chapter 8	An Eerie and Diabolical Truce	152
Chapter 9	The Night Party	162
Chapter 10	The Small Observation Unit	182
Chapter 11	Another Bombardment	199
Chapter 12	In the Morning Mist	215
Author's Note		239

CHAPTER 1

A PICTURE OF WONDERFUL CAMARADERIE AND DELIGHT (NORTH AFRICA, 1941)

The truck rumbled across the desert road towards the British Commonwealth's front line. The front line where the Axis powers would be ready and waiting. The front line that was constantly changing. Sometimes for the better, sometimes for the worse. No one in the back of the three-ton lorry knew or cared where the front line might be at such a time. They had been happy in the Port of Alexandria, but now the commitments of the war had to be answered with active duty. It was the final sing-song for the lads. All fine men of their respective tank crews.

'A grand gathering of Matilda tanks awaits our attention, now, boys,' shouted Sergeant McGrew in his harsh Belfast accent. 'Lieutenant Gibbon will want us all to look after them good and proper, so he will.'

'That's for sure,' replied Billy O'Hara, a fellow Ulsterman from County Antrim.

'We'll do him proud, Serge,' replied Meadows in his brash cockney accent.

'We'll keep them good and proper,' added Nuts and Bolts – the highly strung driver of the first commander Lieutenant Gibbon's tank crew.

'Indeed, we will,' agreed Impett the gunner with Lieutenant Gibbon's tank.

'Well, Twinkle Toes, we know that,' replied Meadows, knowing that Impett hated the nickname. 'You along with our Nuts and Bolts are Lieutenant Gibbon's shiny boots boys. Keep the breech and the seats nicely polished, do you?'

'Jealousy!' yelled Nuts and Bolts. 'Out and out jealousy. That's the mark of it. Take no notice, Twinkle Toes—'

'Impett! I'm surprised at you calling me that,' corrected aggrieved Trooper Impett.

'Sorry, Impett.' Nuts and Bolts looked at the rest of the troop holding on to the various grips as the Bedford lorry rumbled over the desert track. 'See what you made me do? Did you see?' He turned back to Impett and repeated, 'Sorry, Impett.'

'That's alright, Nuts and Bolts. I know what this lot are like,' said Impett.

O'Hara spoke next. 'If you're sorry about saying Twinkle Toes, how comes Twinkle Toes still calls you Nuts and Bolts?'

'What!' Nuts and Bolts replied, his voice rising in erratic excitement. 'How our little crew operate is down to us. Nothing to do with the rest of you.'

Whoops of laughter and leg-pulling ensued as Nuts and Bolts continued to try and make his point, his excitement growing as he became more erratic.

'Calm down, Nuts and Bolts,' added Meadows. 'Stop straining like that! You'll have an accident.'

'Accident? Accident? How will I have an accident?' Nuts and Bolts' face was glowing red with frustration.

'You'll mess yourself if you're not careful,' added Louis with pretentious concern.

Nuts and Bolts sighed. 'Bloody coarse, you lot are. No refinement like Twink—Impett and me.'

'Do you act that way inside the tank with Lieutenant Gibbon?' Sergeant McGrew said, laughing at the antics. 'Nuts and Bolts, you seem very erratic indeed, that's for sure.'

'He always is,' said Meadows. 'A complete fusspot that we're all happy to lose to Lieutenant Gibbon. With Twinkle Toes, otherwise known as Impett, the platoon is complete. The only person missing is Lieutenant Gibbon.'

Sergeant McGrew said, 'He has gone before us to inspect the new Matilda tanks we'll be using.'

O'Hara looked a little solemn. 'It's a shame we've finished our leave period. I could have done with another fortnight.'

Louis chuckled. 'I would have gone for a year or two.'

'Well, at least I got to see one of my favourite flicks before setting off,' said young Harry Edwards, bouncing on the bench of the Bedford lorry as the vehicle made its way across the bumpy desert terrain. The lad from Ramsgate in Kent was a keen and likeable new addition to the troop.

'What, Shirley Temple in *The Littlest Rebel*? I would have thought you'd be a bit more of a geezer, young Harry?' Fred 'Caterpillar' Miller grinned at the young trooper. He was a big man with thick black hair beneath his beret. Hair that he was constantly being told to get cut.

'Caterpillar Miller's hair grows very quickly and so do his balls when there's some ribbing to be done,' said Trooper Edwards, grinning in his good-natured, youthful way.

'You know me, young Edwards. You know me too well.' Caterpillar Miller chuckled. He also had big bushy eyebrows that met in the middle. These formed a huge single eyebrow that looked like a giant hairy caterpillar lying between the tops of his eyes and his suntanned forehead, hence his nickname, Caterpillar Miller.

'I'm surprised you didn't want an ice cream during the show, Harry, that's for sure,' added O'Hara, giggling like a naughty school lad.

Young Harry Edwards smiled back at the good-natured joshing. 'I'm the complete glutton for that song she sang.'

'What, "Polly Wolly Doodle"?' added Meadows, pretending to look repulsed.

'Get out of it,' said Harry, laughing, 'you were singing along too. You liked it just as much as the rest of us.'

Sergeant McGrew smiled at the trusting eighteen-year-old. 'It's all a big thrill for you, young Edwards. Is it not so, now?'

The young trooper grinned and replied, 'Well, Serge, so far North Africa has been a learning experience. I wouldn't want to repeat some of the antics…'

A roar of laughter erupted from the other troopers in their oversized shorts and scruffy khaki shirts complete with black berets.

'No, you wouldn't want to do that again,' replied Sergeant McGrew, chuckling. He took his beret off and playfully swiped the lad over the head with it. 'Not with that big-titted old brass who made off with yer wallet, now. That's for sure, young Edwards.'

There was more laughter and further woops of delight as all on board the lorry enjoyed teasing the easy-to-like Trooper Edwards and his easy-going way. He hadn't a malicious streak in him, but he was being trained and conditioned, like the rest, to kill people. The campaign in North Africa had rapidly become a bitter and wicked theatre of the war.

'Never take your wallet full and loaded into a brothel, young Edwards,' said Louis Donnell, chuckling, the black man with a cockney accent, much the same as Meadows', except a little squeakier. Louis took off his thick brown-rimmed spectacles to clean while displaying his sparkling white teeth in a broad smile.

'Louis has a point there, young Edwards,' added O'Hara. 'The only thing you keep loaded in the brothels is yer ball bag.'

'The bloke has a point there, Harry,' added Caterpillar Miller.

'You do like to get your two pennies' worth in, don't you, Caterpillar?' Edwards grinned cheekily.

More rudely drawn humour accompanied the group of troopers as the rickety lorry rumbled over the desert terrain. Everyone was laughing. Everyone was happy. Sergeant McGrew was pleased to see his lads so at ease. Now was a little golden moment. Who knew what the next day might bring? Harry Edwards had fitted in with the group nicely. Upon arrival, like all recruits, he had been given the run around with all sorts of pranks, but the lad had taken the jokes in good humour and even thrown a few quick-witted replies. The lad was a good one, that was for sure, in Sergeant McGrew's opinion.

Harry Edwards nodded at the troopers sitting inside the shade of the lorry's canvas covering and chuckled as he took the good-natured antics. 'Well, it's a lesson not lost on me. I thought it was too good to be true.'

'Did you not get yer pecker felt before the old brass made off with yer wallet?' enquired O'Hara.

'Oh yeah, she swiped me wallet while I was sleeping it off,' replied Trooper Edwards.

'All you can do is put it down to experience, young Edwards,' added Louis with another striking grin of snow-white teeth against his dark skin. He put his cleaned spectacles back on and his eyes magnified, almost as though they might pop out.

'A lesson well and truly learned, Mr Donnell. Mark my words.' Trooper Edwards grinned while lighting a cigarette and offered the pack to Louis, pointing to the rest of the troop.

'Well then,' added Sergeant McGrew, 'should we not have a little sing-song of young Edwards' favourite ballad, now? After all, it was a rather bonny number, for sure.'

'Why not, indeedy?' agreed Louis with another broad and gleaming smile.

'That one wins my vote, but young Edwards has to start it off. After all, you have said it's one of your favourite flicks. The Shirley Temple words and not the other ones.'

'Are the other ones dirty then?' asked O'Hara.

'No,' said Edwards, laughing, 'just different lyrics that I've seen. I know the sets of lyrics off by heart, the Shirley Temple lyrics from the flick and the other ones on a music sheet I bought from an old music shop back home in Ramsgate.'

'What ones do you like the best, young Edwards?' asked Sergeant McGrew.

Trooper Harry Edwards grinned at them all. 'No contest. *The Littlest Rebel*, every time for me.'

'Let's give it some large then.' Louis had got out his spoons and was making ready to start.

O'Hara had got out his mouth organ and was wiping it against his dusty shorts in readiness, waiting for a nod from the spoon man, Louis.

'How about that, now?' Sergeant McGrew beamed, looking at young Edwards. 'A nice cat's chorus to help you along yer way.'

Louis called out, 'One, two, three…'

Immediately O'Hara and Louis got a kindly rhythm going for Trooper Harry Edwards to do his Trooper Harry Edwards' thing.

Oh! I eat watermelon and I have for years,
sing Polly-wolly-doodle all the day;

I like watermelon but it wets my ears,
sing Polly-wolly-doodle all the day.

Maybe grass tastes good to a moo cow's mouth,
sing Polly-wolly-doodle all the day;
But I like chicken 'cause I'm from the south,
sing Polly-wolly-doodle all the day.

Fare-thee well,
Fare-thee well,
Mister gloom be on your way.

Sergeant McGrew looked at all his great lads as the song went on. He was overjoyed by the good spirit of it all. The seasoned sergeant knew what was in store and he supposed it would be very testing indeed. But for now, they were all in a little bubble of happiness. A wonderful picture of camaraderie and delight. An alcove of joy that would always be out there somewhere. Somewhere in eternity. Forever happy, forever singing, 'Polly-wolly-doodle all the day'. There was the young, fresh-faced Harry Edwards, full of joy and life. Eighteen years of age and at one with the world and his friends. What a pleasing picture it made to all of the troop on that very fine day. Could there ever be a better sight of camaraderie and a bonnier young lad?

Twenty-four hours later, McGrew was coming to. He was dazed and in pain, but the heat and the confined space were gone. Now it was the warm air of the desert. His hands and legs were blackened and charred. Someone was pulling him away from the burning Matilda tank. His rescuer was saying something. He sensed it but couldn't hear what was being said. A constant, high-pitched noise buzzed within his traumatised ears. How bad was he injured? His legs were numb and useless. All McGrew could do was watch helplessly while he was dragged further from the burning tank. He dropped his gaze to his towing heels – dusty and dirty boots in a position of ten to two. He noted the furrows his heels left over the desert sand in bemusement. He tried hard to remember what had happened. Then recollection, slow and dreadful.

They had been hit by an Italian field gun. He could vaguely remember Meadows shouting the alarm. Then he jolted back from his dazed pondering. The droning noise in his beat-up ears abruptly stopped and his hearing began to function again. He was back in the dreadful circumstance before him. Now there was distant screaming! It was coming from the flaming tank.

'Oh, good God in Heaven!' he mumbled. 'No, no, no! Please don't let it be so.'

Hideous, agonising shrieks of pain. A trooper burning to death within the confines of the burning Matilda tank, where the wicked flames began to engulf every part of the stricken vehicle. The wretched, high-pitched wails of a man reduced to such shocking cries for his mother as he roasted alive. Diabolical, unearthly squeals coming from the horrifying and burning testament, like a screaming infant begging to be gone.

Suddenly all went silent. An even more guilt-ridden sense kicked in, an abstract calm that mocked all survivors through the crackle of the flaming wreck. Immediate hush. The screams, thankfully gone. The eerie quiet of a tortured soul released and a sudden emptiness that was haunting with chilling gratitude. A shameful thanks that the agonised calls of the departed soul were no longer there. All that remained was the flaming tank with the receding, calm echo of a dreadful memory. Something no survivor would ever forget. The wretched life that was taken during the throws of outright burning agony. Now it was the wicked silence that haunted McGrew and the continuing sight of the burning Matilda tank, a devouring fire that branded its image into the sergeant's memory.

'Sorry, Serge. I'm so sorry. We couldn't get the poor sod out!' It was the sympathetic cockney accent of Meadows, the trooper pulling McGrew away from the stricken and burning Matilda tank.

'Oh my God! Not poor little Harry Edwards. For the love of God, tell me it's not so, Meadows?'

Meadows stopped at a safe distance from the burning wreck. 'Harry's gone, Serge. We were hit by an Italian field gun. We rumbled straight into the bastard at point-blank range, or as good as. That's them over there. Miller, Donnell and O'Hara got the bastards. I don't know where Lieutenant Gibbon's tank's gone. Nuts and Bolts with Impett at the gun have charged on ahead.'

Just by a rise in the terrain, there were some sandbags and the burning wreckage of a field gun. Two bodies lay in the sand – those of Italian artillery men by their burning field gun.

'I think it's one of those Obice da seventy-five stroke eighteen medello things from the manual…'

'Meadows! I don't give a dead rat's backside what the bloody gun is called. It's a ruddy enemy field gun and it's killed our little Harry Edwards. That's all I can think about. It reduced the poor little sod to a screaming wreck. Did you hear him pleading to get out of that burning bloody tank? I keep seeing his face from yesterday in the truck, God bless him. There he is, when I look up into the sky, out there in that little alcove – in my mind's eye and eternity. That bundle of innocence singing "Polly-wolly-doodle all the day". The wicked bastards. An eighteen-year-old with everything in front of him. This is the biggest shitshow of all time, Meadows. And do you know what?'

'What, Serge?' Meadows placed a comforting hand on his sergeant's shoulder as the man sat there on the desert floor, burnt and dishevelled from his near-death experience.

'There'll still be other shitshows in the future when this one is all over. More killing and another war to end all wars.' McGrew looked over at the two dead artillery men next to the burning equipment and the wrecked field gun.

Meadows could fathom McGrew's train of thought. 'Eyeties have paid a heavy price too, Serge. Not that this is any consolation. We've lost little Harry Edwards.'

'I wonder what it will be like for all their mothers and fathers too, as well as for Harry Edwards' family. The Eyeties must go through the same agony, especially where loved ones are concerned.' Sergeant McGrew was staring at the dead enemy and was willing himself back to the dreadful world of fire, death and the prospect of more killing to come. It had to be confronted and he needed to go with the way things were.

'It will be horrendous for them all, Serge. Sod that. We can't let Harry's people know the manner of his death. It would be wicked.'

Sergeant McGrew put his hand on Meadows', the very hand resting on his shoulder. Now he tried to console Meadows.

'We'll not be doing it like that, Meadows, that's for sure. Our Harry was taken quickly and bravely. The lad had courage and no one ever deserves to go like that.'

'It was bloody evil, Serge.'

The sudden rumble of tank tracks caught their attention. They were those of a Matilda tank and for the first time, far-off booms of battle could be heard all about them, as though they had burst through the bubble of uncanny fires and contemplative thought. In front of the returning Matilda walked two Italian prisoners, each holding up his hands and looking very nervous. Their light-beige jackets and leggings were burnt and shoddy after recent combat.

The tank stopped and the cupola hatch opened to reveal O'Hara staring back at them. He had a triumphant grin on his face.

'These two Eyeties tried to do a runner,' he said.

'Well, it does make sense when your gun is taken out,' added Sergeant McGrew. He struggled to get up, aided by Meadows. The concussion was wearing off but he still had the beginnings of a headache.

'They got poor little Harry Edwards,' added Meadows.

'What!' exclaimed O'Hara, shocked. Emotions ran riot across his face and he stared down at the two nervous Italian prisoners. He reached into the tank and pulled out a revolver.

'Don't you even go thinking about it, O'Hara,' bellowed Sergeant McGrew as he walked forward. 'My God, I'm bloody disappointed in you, O'Hara. So, help me God, I am. I expected better from my fellow countryman.'

'But they killed young Edwards. Why not kill the sods? No one will know.' O'Hara was calming down even as he was saying the words he didn't mean.

'The Eyeties have lost two of their mates too, Billy,' said Meadows, nodding towards the two dead Italian artillery men by the wrecked cannon.

Sergeant McGrew had pulled out his hand gun and inadvertently made the two Italian prisoners more nervous. He had to abate their fears. He gesticulated for them to lower their hands.

'Put your hands down now, lads. It's all over for you boys now. No more fighting.'

As the Italian artillery men slowly lowered their hands, one of them tried to speak. He pointed at their two dead comrades.

'*Per favore, posso controllare che i miei amici siano morti?*' he asked.

Louis was climbing down from the Matilda with O'Hara as he said, 'I think they're asking to check and see if their friends are dead.'

The two Italians nodded as though understanding what Louis was translating.

'Tell them they can,' added McGrew.

Louis looked at the Italians, nodded and said, '*Sì*.'

McGrew screwed his face up and replied, '*Sì*? Is that it, Louis? Bloody hell, I could have said that. I thought you had some understanding of Italian.'

Louis chuckled and pulled off his thick brown-rimmed glasses and began to clean them.

'No, I'm just going on guess work and gestures, Serge,' he replied in his squeaky voice.

Sergeant McGrew sighed despondently as he stood there with Meadows. Both bloody and burnt. Also stricken with remorse and very unsettled by the dreadful circumstances of young Harry Edwards' violent and horrific death. All of them were coming back down to earth with nervous tremors. McGrew's hands shook as he tried to put a cigarette in his mouth.

'I've seen death before, Meadows,' he stuttered. 'But this one is a little more gut-wrenching than most.'

'I know, Serge. Harry was a smashing lad. Everyone liked him,' added Meadows.

McGrew pulled nervously on his cigarette. 'I've a feeling we're going to be experiencing a lot more of this type of thing. I think there's a long way to go before this shitshow is over.'

'I know this is difficult, Serge. But we must go on,' added Meadows.

O'Hara agreed. 'Our Meadows is right, Serge. That's for sure.'

McGrew smiled at his one fellow Irishman of the troop. O'Hara often liked to add the phrase 'that's for sure' at the end of his sentences. A minor little thing, but for the moment it amused the older sergeant as he realised, he often said it too. A small thing – something familiar and comforting concerning the troop of good men.

Around them, the conflict continued, though they had no idea who was winning or losing. Their small troop were in a quandary and they had destroyed a field gun position and taken prisoners.

'I think I shall try not to get attached to the new troopers they send us. I think this sort of thing might become a regular occurrence,' said McGrew.

'This is how our metal will become tempered, Serge,' replied Louis.

'Aye,' agreed O'Hara. 'The shape of things to come, that's for sure.'

The two Italians had walked over to check upon their comrades, and now looked up and slowly shook their heads at Trooper Louis and Sergeant McGrew. They reserved a slightly more cautious look for O'Hara and Meadows, who were both pointing guns at them. The Matilda's machine gun was also aimed in their direction – no doubt Miller had them squarely in sight in case they tried to run.

Slowly, both Italian soldiers stood up. McGrew gestured with his hand for them to approach. Each soldier complied and came forward. The sergeant held out a water bottle and the soldiers received the offer with gratitude.

'*Grazie,*' they both replied.

Meadows offered each of them a cigarette and again, the soldiers were grateful. One moment they were trying to kill one another, the next they were trying to indulge one another in small talk. Each had lost friends. Each was filled with great remorse. All of them were war weary, yet there would be so much of the war left for them all.

CHAPTER 2

THE BURNT-OUT STURMGESCHÜTZ (DUTCH–GERMAN BORDER – 1945)

It was a bitterly cold morning in the first week of February. Scattered clumps of January snow remained everywhere across the freezing fields. But the country lanes had become a slushy mire, distant and narrow conduits where military traffic slowly moved along in convoy. It all seemed sluggish. But bit by bit and by hook or by crook, the gradual Allied advance across Northern Europe continued.

There was a temporary pontoon bridge stretching across the river and another road running alongside the opposite bank. All traffic was crossing the bridge, leaving the road on the opposite bank empty beyond the crossing. Perhaps there was some knowledge of an enemy patiently waiting on the opposite side of the narrow river, where a line of trees offered ample cover – a hidden enemy, waiting for any Allied traffic that went along that route beyond the bridge.

Trooper John Meadows whistled with awe at the sight of the wreckage and then spoke to the new trooper standing next to him. 'We've come all the way from Normandy and we're now on the German border. At least I think we're at the border in this section. Now, here we are, just over eight months on from D-Day and nicely into nineteen forty-five. We must be just inside the National Socialist nation of the thousand-year Reich. Who knows for sure? We've come via the fields and left out the roads over the last few miles so we haven't seen any signposts while motoring across the frozen pastures. Leave the approach roads to those silly sods down there. They all seem to want to cross over to this side of the river.' He turned his gaze back to the approaching forces.

The new recruit, they all called Wingnut, replied, 'I've been told there are plenty of signs along the road written in dodgy English by Jerry. Warning us that we are entering the so-called Fatherland. By the way, you're beginning to sound like Déjà vu McGrew and O'Hara when you keep saying "for sure". You might be having some of that Irish rub off on you?'

'When did I say that?' asked Meadows, unable to take his eyes off the young lad's big ears that splayed out each side of his big cherub-faced head.

'When you said "who knows" and then you added, "for sure".'

Meadows replied, 'That's in a completely different context.' He started chuckling at the wicked thought of Wingnut looking like a trophy cup with his jug-handle ears. The leg-pulling of the troop had abated by now. Wingnut, the durable recruit had ridden the storm with ease. He even accepted his nickname. Though Meadows didn't think the lad liked it.

Wingnut looked thoughtful. 'Oh, okay then. As for our location, I think you're right. We're just inside Germany by now. If not, this is the border and that cluster of trees across that basin, just on the other side of that little stream flowing into the main river, that's certainly where Adolf lives. Well, he doesn't live right there but he must have a few stylish gaffs further inside the country.'

'Well,' replied Meadows as he ambled closer to the burnt-out Sturmgeschütz III. 'To indulge your first statement about my use of "for sure", you can't be around such men for over four years and not have some of their ways rub off on you. Even though my context was different.'

'I know, you just said that. Déjà vu and O'Hara repeat themselves too.'

Meadows ignored the mild rebuke from the cocky new recruit and continued, 'It certainly has been a long hard slog getting this far. And now here is Germany on a cold winter's day in February. Bloody hell, it's definitely been a long hard slog, Wingnut. Let's hope we're getting close to the finishing line of this grand shitshow. The war must end this year, surely.'

'Déjà vu calls the war a shitshow too,' added Wingnut, trying to lend emphasis to Meadows becoming more Irish than English in his demeanour.

Meadows turned from his inspection of the wrecked enemy tank to look directly at Wingnut with a raised eyebrow. 'You'll find a wide range of people on both sides of this conflict referring to this said war as a "shitshow", Wingnut. We never invented the word. It's a fashionable figure of speech that's been doing the rounds from start to finish. Also, do yourself a little favour and don't let our Sergeant McGrew hear you referring to him as Déjà vu, not until you have settled in a little bit more. The sergeant's always a little off with the new lads. He doesn't like to get attached straight away. Seen too many young men die. It's a superstition of his nowadays, and with good reason. He's seen it all before. As for "Déjà vu", it's not a well-intentioned nickname. At best, it's sympathetic. Trust us, Wingnut, this troop is full of sad anecdotes, some funny ones too. But the sad ones weigh heavy on the sergeant sometimes. He rolls with the shitshow but he doesn't like it.'

'I never heard the shitshow thing before I was sent here,' replied Wingnut, nodding his acceptance with an innocent smile.

Again, Meadows raised another amused eyebrow and shook his head slightly while trying not to laugh. 'Wingnut, you've only been here four days. You're still green, mate. We've all been green once. At the moment, you are, lad. As I've said, this troop has been together four years plus. You've replaced our Trooper Marks. He got carted off with appendicitis, the lucky bastard.'

'I don't suppose he felt very lucky,' replied Wingnut, taking out a packet of cigarettes and offering one to Meadows, who thankfully accepted.

'By the time he has convalesced and ready to come back, I reckon this shitshow might be over. Don't forget, Jerry's also fighting the Russians from the other side of their glorious thousand-year Reich,' Meadows replied while leaning forward with the cigarette between his lips to receive the covered light from Wingnut.

Meadows put his hands back in the pockets of his khaki pixie suit as he continued to amble around the burnt-out wreck of the Sturmgeschütz, his smouldering cigarette hanging from his lips. Wingnut followed in the same cocky stance with his hands inside the pockets of his worn khaki pixie suit, almost as if he was trying to emulate the veteran trooper. The black tank beret with cap badge was neatly fashioned upon his head in the same way as Meadows'.

'I've noticed you lads don't swear the way other troopers do,' added Wingnut. 'Other units are full of foul-mouthed four-letter words. You lot talk like you're all in a film matinee.'

Meadows nodded and replied, 'There are only two words we do not use. They are four letters – one beginning with F and the other with C. Again, our Sergeant McGrew can't stand the use of these particular words and he spent some time screaming and scolding it out of us in North Africa. That's a whim on the sergeant's part. We indulge him on that. Believe me, Wingnut – you can say things like, bloody, blinking, ruddy and so forth. We even use the word shit, but the F and C words are right out in our Molly or any other tank we're using. If you want to see our Déjà vu McGrew throw an angry fit, use the F word or the C word. Trust me, you'll not do it again. These swear words are taboo – completely and utterly.'

'Point taken,' replied Wingnut. 'They are horrible words.'

Meadows smiled at Wingnut. He seemed a decent new recruit. He then turned his attention back to the burnt-out wreck before them. 'I wonder what troop mullered this gorgeous little tart.'

'So, we can say the word tart then?' asked Wingnut.

Meadows raised an eyebrow. 'Well of course we can or I wouldn't have ruddy said it, would I? Only the F and the C words are out of bounds.'

'Point taken,' replied the recruit.

The veteran trooper studied the shell hole just below the side vendor and the top rollers on the burnt-out Sturmgeschütz.

'Well, someone touched this bitch up good and proper,' he said with a tone of admiration.

'I heard it was a Polish troop. In a Cromwell tank, just like ours,' answered Wingnut.

'Really, where did you hear that?'

'That group of Canadian soldiers told me about half an hour ago.'

'Oh, they must have seen it then. They got here yesterday by all accounts and there's a Polish troop here. I've seen some of their troopers about.'

'I didn't think a Cromwell could take out a Sturmgeschütz III,' added Wingnut disbelievingly. 'The shell would hit the armour at an angle and bounce off. Or so I've been told.'

'It can take one of these things if the range and circumstance is right,' replied Meadows. 'Most shells can penetrate at the right place and range somewhere, especially if the angle is good. Below the top rollers and track at the side here. Well, that isn't going to stop a shell – an AP would do this old girl up a treat. Look at her! Well and truly touched up.'

'Really,' Wingnut replied. He was interested in such things as ballistics. 'Have you blokes ever had a Tiger tank? I know you've come here via the desert campaign and Italy. You must have come across Tiger tanks before? I'm told they're hard to take out.'

'Tigers are difficult front-on. You need to get side-on and at a close enough range. Jerry, in his Tiger, isn't going to let us do that now, is he? And of course, we have seen Tiger tanks. Most were burnt-out ones in France, at the beginning of the campaign. I think many of these were taken out by aircraft. The active ones were at a distance and we liked it that way. Leave those beasts to the air force.

'We saw more Tiger tanks head-on in North Africa and Italy. Trust me, that isn't a pretty sight. None of us felt privileged or lucky to see such an awe-inspiring tank. We got unhorsed by one once. Got nearly killed by such bloody tarts. Trust me, Wingnut, you don't want one of those big old brasses coming on to you, because they do, you know. Good and proper. Got unhorsed by one of these Sturmgeschütz bastards too. That's a piece of work too, mate. An assault gun on tracks. Believe me when I say such things. Forget all your romantic stories about Tigers and King Tiger tanks. They're gorgeous big "bugger off" ladies. Ladies that are well and truly out of our humble league. The Marlene Dietrich of the tank world.'

'That good, aye?' Wingnut laughed. He enjoyed Meadows' way of personification. 'All British or American tanks are loveable old horses. Not up to much but they mean well. All German tanks are tempting fire-breathing bitches. This is the way of your simplistic world – Jerry tanks are naughty ladies of ill repute and fantasy, gorgeous actresses that no ordinary man would get a chance at.'

Meadows grinned as he looked to the burnt-out Sturmgeschütz wreck. 'Too right, mate. And Marlene – our Tiger tank – is an elegant lady. She doesn't put it about much. She plays hard to get, the little teaser. There're only a few gorgeous bitches about nowadays. However, these big old brasses, that are not tanks – your Jerry Sturmgeschütz and the eighty-eight flak guns – they're the cheap, wicked bitches to look out for. They'll take you for a ride good and proper. Nasty big tarts that like to hide in hedgerows and ambush you with a quick shell and then bugger off to another position to wait for another of our nags to come galloping along the lane. These mounted artillery guns get more of us than Jerry's smashing, but over-engineered, tanks. Your sexy Marlene Dietrich Tigers are the gorgeous babes of the tank world. They're great pieces of work with bottoms you might want to pinch. But, as I've said, there're not enough of them.'

Again, Meadows turned his attention back to the burnt-out Sturmgeschütz and nodded. 'Shit loads of these bastards, though. Look at it. A huge field gun on an old Panzer III chassis. It gets the job done. Jerry has built thousands of them. The one that got us in Tunisia had the shorter barrel and it was obviously desert yellow. This has white winter camouflage and a longer, more powerful "bugger off" gun.'

Meadows grinned appreciatingly as he examined the wrecked enemy killing machine and scrutinised the various shell impact holes a little more intently. The fact that a Polish Cromwell tank did the deed interested him. He was fascinated by the enemy vehicle. He could see it was an adaptation – a field gun mounted upon an obsolete tank chassis with protective armour built around it. It was simplistic, yet splendid.

'So, our company never took out a Tiger then,' muttered Wingnut rhetorically. There was a note of disappointment in his tone.

'Nope, never,' replied Meadows. 'Only ever seen them at a distance in North Africa and Italy. Even saw the one that mullered our Churchill in Italy as it was moving off. That bloody Marlene did a right old number on us. Off she rumbled, shaking her arse like a high-class bitch walking off a Broadway stage show. We got laid good and proper. I remember Louis complaining about it as we watched the Jerry tart roll off into the distance. If ever we got a big "bugger off" kiss, that was it. We, in turn, have taken out artillery units, armoured vehicles like the Marder and a few of their half-tracks. A Panzer IV as well, on one occasion – oh, and a Panzer III in Tunisia, as I recall. But then there's the eighty-eight flak gun. Now there's a piece of work you'll do well to fear. The Jerry eighty-eight flak gun is another nasty bitch. You'll certainly know when one of their shells strikes your tank – or rather, you won't. I'm more scared of those eighty-eights than our Jerry Sturmgeschütz we have here. And, just for the record, this Sturm III is still a tasty piece of work.'

'I've been told about the eighty-eight flak guns. The Canadian soldiers reckon they're motorised now and are more easily manoeuvred about,' replied Wingnut, like the willing pupil.

'Jerry has had their eighty-eights on wheels for bleeding ages. They say that this type of gun is not as accurate when on a wheeled platform, but I think that's a load of bollocks.'

'But you've never destroyed a Tiger tank?' Wingnut repeated, as though Meadows may have forgotten.

'No, Wingnut, lad. Trust me, I would remember. The Panzer III and IV, as I said – and, we did get an Italian M13 medium tank in Tunisia, as well. I forgot about that one.'

'I've never heard of one of those,' replied Wingnut. 'I've heard it said the Eyeties were not that good.'

'Well, to be more precise, the Italian tank is called a Fiat Ansaldo M13 40. We captured a few. I heard the Australians put them to good use while fighting the desert campaign. As for the Eyeties not being that good, don't believe all you hear. They had bad equipment out in North Africa but their artillery units were sound. We got unhorsed by one of their field guns once. In fact, it was the first time we were unhorsed. Lost a good lad too. He was much like you, Wingnut. It affected the sergeant badly. In many ways, that's why he is abrupt with new recruits at first. He mellows once he gets used to you.'

'I heard the Aussies are a rough lot,' added Wingnut, preferring to move away from the topic of troopers like him getting killed.

'They are, Wingnut,' said Meadows. 'But don't fret about it, lad. They're on our side, you know. And they dish out some serious large to Jerry.'

'So do the Poles.' Wingnut chuckled, nodding to the wrecked Sturmgeschütz.

'You can certainly say that again, Wingnut, me old mucker. They got this lovely juicy tart from the side. If you're going for a Sturmgeschütz III, it's always best to hit it side-on – square-on – and at the right distance. A good ninety-degree impact angle against the lighter armour of this flank, hence the two shell holes below the vendor and the upper track. And a third has smashed the sprocket and track. You can see that the Polish gunner must have been close enough to aim well and at spots he knew were weak areas – this particular one knew his onions when it comes to placing his shells inside this saucy little teaser. Quality troopers, I would say.'

Wingnut raised an eyebrow. 'Your personification of loose ladies for German tanks is continuously amusing. It's as though such vehicles are gorgeous but way out of your league, like ladies, and you're resentful and jealous because you couldn't pull one in a night club.'

'Yeah,' Meadows agreed with a distant stare. He was contemplating Wingnut's words. There was an element of truth there. 'With my luck on the lady front, I'd probably pull a universal Bren carrier. They aren't up to much.'

Wingnut chuckled. 'Oh, poor me. Pour me another drink, please.'

'Mine will be a large Scotch with ice,' said Meadows, laughing good-humouredly. He often displayed his sense of humour by making himself seem like a victim. The man had a comical knack and was easy, enjoyable company, a typical trooper who got on with things in a cheerful way.

Wingnut turned his attention back to the destroyed Sturmgeschütz with a look of admiration. 'The *Zimmerit* has flaked off around the front, near the scissor scope. There, coming out of the cupola. It's all burnt. Must have been a fire inside. The Polish gunner was definitely on the ball. A good shot with a loader that was quick and calm, I would reckon.'

'My loading is quick. We'd heard you were a good gunner back at training. Maybe we might get to do this before the shitshow is over?'

Wingnut smiled enthusiastically. 'What, you and me doing a number as good as this on our own Sturmgeschütz? That would be something.'

Meadows nodded his agreement. 'Our Polish lads must have been close to score hits of this consistency. I mean, almost pinpoint without Jerry knowing the enemy was on him. It had to be like slapping a fat tart's enormous arse with a banjo.'

Wingnut pondered Meadows' words as he tried to visualise the metaphorical concept. 'So, this is the *Zimmerit* layer of concrete protective stuff. I've heard a lot about this. It gives some form of protection?' He was running his hand over the hard-ridged substance. 'Bloody hell, the base of the gun barrel has this huge concrete blob around it. Reminds me of a giant wasp nest I once saw in our garden shed.'

'It does,' replied Meadows, laughing. 'The *Zimmerit* ridges are to stop magnetic and sticky bombs. It means a soldier could never attach a magnetic mine over the *Zimmerit*. The magnet needs to touch metal to stay in place. With this stuff, the mine can't stick, it just falls to the floor.'

'Did the Polish tank knock the *Zimmerit* off when the shell struck?' asked Wingnut as he scrutinised areas where the ridged sealant had flaked off to expose the metal armour beneath.

'I'm not sure. But if I had to guess, I would say no. I think the tank was close enough to aim at the exposed and thinner metal plate below the vendors and the *Zimmerit* had already flaked off in other conflicts. Trust me, Wingnut, those Polish lads had to be close, mate. Very close indeed.'

'Again, I have to say, cracking shooting,' replied Wingnut in awe.

'Do you reckon your gunnery is up to it, Wingnut?'

Wingnut sighed in satisfaction. 'Well, I got praise back in training, but I haven't been tested under battle conditions, as you know. I reckon I can make the killing shot though. I'd love to get one of these buggers in my sight.'

'Well, Wingnut, you never know your luck, mate.' Meadows took one last drag on his cigarette and flicked it away. He looked about and tried to work out the trajectory of the shells that hit the vehicle. 'I'm presuming the Jerry wagon was struck here while it had stopped and positioned itself. It's also a well-used machine and I should imagine it has seen a fair deal of campaigning before it came to this fiery end.'

'Right here at this very spot?' asked Wingnut.

'That's right. Look, the gun has a clear view of the approach road while hidden behind this hedge –

the scissor scope up and reconnoitring the pontoon bridge. Jerry was preparing for some easy picking.'

Meadows turned and looked in the direction he thought the destroying Allied shells would have been fired from. His vision swept over the line of trees and bushes on the other side of the icy track. He looked about the frozen pathway too.

'There are many tank tracks about, even on the frozen ground, but I'm sure the Polish Cromwell would have been close, hiding in the grove and well covered. Therefore, I think that means our Polish mates were definitely about there.' He pointed to some saplings by a thick hedge.

Wingnut nodded. 'It makes sense. The Sturmgeschütz was outsmarted by a Cromwell doing the Sturmgeschütz thing better than Jerry could, on this occasion.'

The two tank troopers ambled over to the perimeter of the woods and walked around a large holly bush, close to the saplings. Wingnut discarded his cigarette, flicking the smouldering dog-end back onto the frozen earth.

'These are Cromwell tracks,' said Meadows, pointing down to the indentations. He followed the approach track's path, backwards. They came from a deeper position, inside the woods.

'They continue here,' added Wingnut, pleased with himself.

'That's right, Wingnut, the tank would have fired the three shots from here, behind this thicket, and then drove out of the wood and off, by my reckoning, anyway. But feast your little mince pies on this. From here, our lads' tank is square-on to this Jerry's exposed flank. That Polish tank crew must have thought Christmas had come again. I reckon they were parked here, behind the thicket and that Jerry wagon came rumbling along unaware of the Cromwell. They picked their spot and stopped where it's been destroyed. Jerry must have been completely oblivious to the fact that a tank was right on top of them. They were lost in their own little chore of hiding behind their own shrub, too busy sitting there waiting, hoping to take out a few approaching vehicles. Unaware that our Polish mates are sitting here, eating their salami rations and drinking their shitty coffee.'

'I make you right on that one,' said Wingnut, laughing as he formed the picture in his mind's eye. 'There they are, munching and drinking and then along comes Jerry, rumbling to a halt right before their barrel. I think I can picture those Polish lads' excitement when a big juicy target lands plum in their lap.'

Meadows grinned. 'They quickly pump a few shots into the old brass and then break cover and do the big "offsky", as your average Pole might like to term it.'

'Yeah, on this rock-hard frozen path there – its tracks are mixed with other vehicles now. There has been a lot of coming and going, including our Molly mare.' Wingnut looked back at Meadows and frowned. 'Offsky? What's offsky mean?'

'I say, dashed well done, Holmes,' replied Meadows in his film impersonation of Dr Watson. 'Offsky is Polish for off.'

'No, Watson, for your information, off in Polish is not offsky,' replied Wingnut, mimicking a condescending Basil Rathbone manner.

'I say, nothing gets past you, Holmes old chap,' Meadows responded with his well-spoken impersonation of the actor Nigel Bruce.

'My word, we are coming down with a touch of the old Dr Watson.' Wingnut laughed. 'Like the old Basil Rathbone flicks, do you?'

'Wish I was back home in Blighty watching one now. In the Odeon nearby.'

'Well,' responded Wingnut as he walked back out onto the frozen path, 'when this shitshow is over, you'll be able to catch up on a lot of flicks.'

'Do you do the flicks too, Wingnut? You look like you do.'

'Yeah. I like the musicals.'

'Not Shirley Temple in *The Littlest Rebel*?' added Meadows, joking ironically, though the pun was marred by a sad memory.

'How did you guess that? It's one of my favourites of all time, especially that song she sang, "Polly Wolly Doodle". It's one of my favourites.'

'I was hoping you might not have said that,' Meadows replied.

'Oh, why so?' said Wingnut a little confused.

Meadows was hit in the chest by the awful memory of Harry Edwards. A recollection that left him derelict and unnerved. He looked at young Wingnut and felt sad, a terrible revelation dawning. The lad was like young Harry Edwards and with this came a wicked premonition. No! Such a thing was too dreadful to contemplate. It could never happen twice. He would never want to see Sergeant McGrew suffer the vile experience again. The stalwart sergeant who had brought them through the war, watching over them through thick and thin. He spoke to the Almighty, deep inside his thoughts, *Not poor Wingnut as well. Dear God, don't let it happen to Wingnut, not this close to the finishing line. Not again.*

'Are you alright, Meadows?' Wingnut had noticed the deflated look that had come over the veteran trooper.

'Yeah,' Meadows replied, snapping out of his dour pondering. 'Wingnut, let me ask you for a small favour?'

'If I can do it, then fine,' he replied.

'Don't mention anything about that particular film and the song. Especially, the song. It messes Sergeant "Déjà vu" McGrew up. It's all part of the déjà vu thing. It has unkind memories for us all, especially for the sergeant.'

Wingnut frowned, but realised Meadows was deeply sincere in his request. He nodded and replied, 'Of course I will refrain from saying such things about that particular flick.'

'Good lad.' Meadows gave him a friendly pat on the shoulder and then got out his cigarettes and offered one to Wingnut. The brief sombre mood was instantly washed away.

As Wingnut was accepting the light from Meadows, they heard the familiar rumbling of an approaching Cromwell tank. It was coming towards them along the path. Both troopers looked up with cigarettes hanging from lips. It was their tank – little Molly mare, as they called her affectionately. Their little cruiser tank came to a halt before the wrecked Sturmgeschütz. The Cromwell's engine grumbled away in neutral. Molly's dark green painted camouflage was chipped and weathered. In many areas, the underlying dark green was streaked with grimy runs from rainfall. The white star on the front, for aircraft recognition, was an awful slap-and-dab job. The name 'Molly' was on the front of the revolving turret, below and to the left of the long gun barrel. The shabbily handwritten lettering was very amateurish in application, the tiny ineffective white handwriting had been added with a paintbrush. But the muddy surface of splats and grime streaks had obscured the modest lettering more as each day passed.

'Not the best painting of star and name,' muttered Wingnut.

'What's wrong with our little Molly mare?' replied Meadows as though Wingnut had blasphemed.

'I don't think any of you lads would make for painters or decorators in Civvy street,' muttered Wingnut.

Molly's box-shaped turret looked rather ugly with large rivet bolts and faint grime streaks running down from them due to past rainfall. Beside the tank's long gun barrel was a Besa machine gun and just below and on the forward protrusion of the hull was a second Besa machine gun, to the left of the driver's compartment. The nimble tank's neutral running engine suddenly died before Meadows and Wingnut. They watched the driver's hatch open and Louis Donnell's head popped out. His spectacles magnified large brown eyes beneath his neat black beret, the whites of such big bulbous-looking eyes contrasting against his dark brown skin. He greeted them with his usual happy smile, displaying his immaculate, bright white teeth. Louis seemed very vain about his teeth. He looked after them devotedly.

'We came to look at the Sturmgeschütz that the Polish lads are bragging about,' said Louis in his squeaky cockney voice.

O'Hara emerged via the auxiliary gunner's hatch, pushing the side out with a section of metal roof attached. 'Wow! They did a number on that bitch, that's for sure,' he said in his harsh Northern Irish accent.

Both troopers climbed out in enthusiastic interest for the wrecked vehicle by the hedgerow. O'Hara stood at five foot three. A short gruff man, often referred to as the bad-tempered dwarf by troopers in other units, but not by his own tank crew. Molly's men cherished their auxiliary gunner. He was ugly to look at with a previously broken nose and no front teeth – he was the constant brawler with a harsh opinion and a loud voice, not always a desired attribute in a crowded public house when voicing unwanted opinions. With a big comical toothless grin, O'Hara got out his cigarettes and offered one to Louis. He was about to offer Meadows and Wingnut too, but saw they were already smoking.

'So, our Jerry was well and truly stopped by a few of our Cromwell's shells,' Louis said enthusiastically.

'Three shells fired from a Cromwell, good and proper,' replied Wingnut. 'Two below the vendor and track into the exposed and thinner armour plate. Another at the sprocket wheel. They fired all three shots from that thicket there. Or at least, we think the Polish lads did.'

O'Hara and Louis looked to each other and frowned. Then they ambled around the burnt-out wreck to stand next to Meadows and Wingnut to look at the Sturmgeschütz side-on.

'That's four shots, to be sure,' added O'Hara.

'That's right,' agreed Louis.

This time Meadows and Wingnut frowned to one another. They then walked around the back of the blackened fire-stained iron body. The whole rear of the tank was covered by dark soot and fire-damaged metal, the result of an intense blaze. Even the surrounding ground was blackened. They hadn't heeded this particular damage before.

'Bloody hell,' said Wingnut. 'They stuck one in the back too.'

'That makes sense,' added Meadows. 'We missed the shell hole amid the fire damage here. That's four shots in all. Three to the flank and then, as the Polish tank broke from the cover of the wood and hedge, it came around the back and shoved one up the bitch's arse from here.'

'Not a very noble thing to do to the old girl.' Louis tittered.

'Better her than us.' O'Hara laughed. 'We've had one of these bastards pump one into us once, that's for sure. The one in the desert had the old shorter barrel. That tart did a number on your nag though, didn't it, Meadows?'

'Why do you blokes keep talking about these Jerry tanks as though they're whores?' Wingnut asked.

'Because they blooming are, Wingnut. And they're not really tanks, they have no revolving turret. However, they are bloody nasty tarts that will do any bloke up a treat. Don't be getting yourself chatted up by one of these big brasses, that's for sure,' O'Hara replied.

'Too much tart for us to handle in a Cromwell,' added Louis. 'Most of the time.'

'Unless you can get as close as the Poles did without the lady knowing you're about to touch her up. Sometimes a Cromwell has got what it takes at the right range,' said Meadows.

'Perhaps we should carry a bunch of flowers with a ready-to-go candlelit supper arrangement,' added Louis sarcastically. 'Just in case we run into one, unexpectedly.'

Everyone laughed at the notion and the men continued to walk around the destroyed Sturmgeschütz, speculating more and wondering what became of the crew. They discovered no dead bodies inside the vehicle and the sight remained a topic of interest while their sergeant was away from the troop.

'I bet the Poles helped themselves to the ammo boxes inside,' said O'Hara.

'If the fire never set them off while it was burning,' replied Wingnut. 'Why are you interested in the ammo boxes? Jerry calibre is no good to us?'

In unison, O'Hara and Meadows loudly relied, 'Wrong!'

Louis was chuckling and added, 'I've been informed that Jerry calibre machine guns are compatible with our Molly's Besa MGs. Though we've not put that to the test.'

O'Hara climbed up onto the Sturmgeschütz's charred armour and nimbly dropped down through the cupola, past the scissor scope. He was gone for a few seconds and then his head popped back out.

'Nothing inside,' he called down. 'The Poles must have known about the bullet calibre too. The greedy bastards have had the lot. Whoever the crew were, I reckon they must have got out.'

'The Canadians reckon they were all captured,' said Wingnut.

O'Hara climbed back out and jumped down onto the hard ground. He looked along the pathway down towards the basin.

'I reckon this Jerry Sturmgeschütz came up using the incline of the land to conceal itself from our boys in the trees. Look along there. A further dipped curve to the side of that incline, that's for sure. It moves lower and along the main river. This main drop in front runs to that little stream that flows into the wider river, like a twig protruding from a thick tree trunk.'

'That's right,' agreed Meadows. 'Jerry must have known this area might be occupied, yet they still tried to sneak up here along the lower dip, just to get off a few pot shots. But Jerry's approach would have been exposed to our own observers on the other side by the pontoon bridge. There must be loads of lookouts over there. The units here might not see the approach but they would across the river.'

'They probably made the journey under cover of night,' replied Wingnut.

Meadows realised that the recruit was obviously correct in such an assumption and he looked to the others who stared back. Their disapproving raised eyebrows all for him.

'Wingnut!' Meadows said.

'What?' replied the big-eared recruit.

'No one loves a smart-arse.' It was Meadows' way of saying Wingnut was correct.

There followed some good-humoured chuckles and Wingnut grinned, knowing that in a strange way, Meadows had conceded the point to a fledgling crew member.

O'Hara resumed the enjoyable speculation. 'Jerry must have had some arsehole though, that's for sure. Quite a feat to sneak all the way up here.'

'Get medals for being a daft bastard,' added Wingnut.

'Yeah,' agreed Meadows, 'most of the time, posthumously.'

Louis added more theory, indulging their suspicions. 'I reckon they crept up during the bombardment to the north. It was loud and it would drown out the Jerry approach.'

'You lot are a right bunch of Sherlocks today, aren't you?' Meadows was feeling outplayed by the entire debate, but the warm camaraderie was there and everyone was in a fine mood.

The sound of distant aircraft captured their attention. It was also of interest to the numerous Canadian and Polish troopers from other tank and infantry units – their scattered numbers drifted out of the woods to watch the diving aircraft. All could hear the craft, but none could see it.

Before the Allied Army onlookers was the lower basin. A long narrow line of trees ran along their side of the river. On the other side was meadow-land and odd scattered trees. There was a sudden commotion as many soldiers lined the edge of the steep hill that dropped down towards the tributary below.

'Well, it's certainly tickled their fancy,' said Meadows, watching the scattered groups of Allied troops.

Louis turned and watched the clusters of men as they looked out over the land towards the north east. They could still hear the aircraft but still, none could see it.

'It's one of ours, that's for sure,' said O'Hara.

'A Typhoon, I think,' added Louis.

'It's diving,' said Meadows.

'All I can see is a distant horse and cart right over there.' Wingnut pointed to a tiny speck of movement in the distance.

'By that small cluster of trees over where the land is beginning to rise again,' said Louis, also pointing.

'I can see it,' answered Meadows.

All looked in the general direction as the aircraft's dive seemed to grow in intensity. Yet still, no one could see the plane.

'It can't be attacking a horse and cart?' Wingnut seemed astounded by the thought.

'We're in Germany and the Allied air force will attack anything that moves, including a horse and cart. It could be used to transport materials to the enemy,' answered Louis.

The noise of the diving aircraft escalated as O'Hara pointed into the sky. 'There she goes – a Typhoon. You were right, Louis.'

'I don't believe it,' said Wingnut in complete shock. 'It's just an old bloke – a farmer doing his thing on the farm. A horse and cart down a country lane.'

The recruit watched in dreaded awe as the diving scream of the Typhoon intensified. He made out the form of an old farmer standing on his cart frantically waving his arms in a pathetic attempt to try and dissuade the pilot from his task.

'Jump for it, you silly sod,' hissed Meadows.

'You aren't going to stop him, you silly bastard – jump!' growled O'Hara.

'No bloody chance, mate.' Louis was talking to the wretched farmer on his cart, knowing the tiny speck could never hear him. It was the voice of exasperation.

The Canadians and the Poles started shouting at the distant spectacle too. All were screaming and imploring the pathetic gesticulating man to jump from the cart and run.

As the aircraft's dive reached its crescendo, a new rhythmic clatter of machine-gun fire spat out within the high-pitched whine. Earth projectile sporadically erupted. A deadly neat line of smoking plumes, several yards before the cart and then straight into it and beyond. The cart, the horse and the frantically gesticulating man were engulfed by the rising geysers of smoke. The Typhoon tore over the site of attack and then began to rise majestically into the grey sky.

'No glory in that,' spat Wingnut, watching the sharp rise of the Typhoon.

'It's war, Wingnut. There's nothing noble about it. This shitshow is a very dirty and nasty business.' Meadows sighed sympathetically.

As the smoke drifted away, they could make out the broken cart and the dead horse. The gesticulating man was not visible amid the destruction.

'It was just a horse and cart,' said Wingnut in disgust. 'What can a poor old farmer with his horse and cart do?'

'Wingnut, any form of transportation is a target,' Meadows countered regrettably.

'Anything that moves can be carrying weapons or supplies to the enemy, Wingnut.' Louis was also unhappy about the dreadful event.

'It's what it is,' added O'Hara. 'German farmers are patriotic and would try to help their troops. Any form of transport can be used. The air force will go for anything moving in enemy territory, that's for sure.'

'This is the nature of things, Wingnut. This is the shitshow. We want to get to the finishing line, and it's just over there somewhere to the east,' added Meadows. He understood the recruit's frustration and disgust. They all did.

'The farmer should have stayed put until we had swept past his farm. Then he could have continued,' said Louis. 'Perhaps he did have weapons or supplies in his cart?'

The incident was over and everyone gradually left the scarp and went back to the woodlands. Back to their various units to await the next part of the campaign.

'Do you honestly believe that, Louis?' Wingnut enquired.

'I'm not sure, but either way the farmer should have abandoned his cart. It was never worth getting shot up for, Wingnut,' answered Louis.

'Oh, aye,' added O'Hara, 'the man should have run off.'

'Perhaps he was trying to save his horse,' Wingnut added.

'Well, more fool him, the silly git,' added Meadows. 'It's done, Wingnut. The farmer and his horse are gone. We can't afford to have issues over such things as this. It's sad but there are so many things that are wrong. It's all part of the shitshow and there are bigger things to concern ourselves with.'

The conversation ended on that note, and the troopers clambered aboard Molly and climbed inside. Within moments, Louis had fired the Merlin engine into life and swung the tank about to drive off and wait with the rest of their platoon.

CHAPTER 3

SUSPICION AND CLICHÉS

Sergeant McGrew returned from his meeting with his superiors. He wasn't happy about the situation ahead of them and made it known to Meadows.

'That new officer of ours, Lieutenant Samson. I'm sure the toff thinks he's that blooming Biblical character, but he doesn't have long hair like Samson. He doesn't realise that the entire army is his big-breasted Delilah, and that Delilah made sure his hair was cut good and short before he put on his uniform. A bloody "top-ho Charlie" who seems blind to pragmatic and essential non-volunteering. A typical overenthusiastic lad of an officer in charge of us all – a fresh-faced nit-wit, just out of nappies. I bet the top brass love the stupid git,' hissed McGrew in his harsh Belfast accent as he blew a stream of cigarette smoke into the afternoon air.

'Has he volunteered us for something stupid to win brownie points?' asked Meadows. 'Christ, let's face it, we've had some wankers along the way. I wish Gibbon was still with us. He was level-headed. But then, you aren't keen on young officers are you, Serge? At the end of the day, they all arrive as "top-ho Charlies" sniffing for brownie points. If they last long enough and get their rude awakening, then they seem to level out. Lieutenant Gibbon did, back in the desert.'

'No, I'm not keen on young officers, John. And I agree about Gibbon, that's for sure,' said McGrew. 'Then he goes and gets himself killed in Italy. That Italian campaign robbed us of some good men. The soft underbelly of Europe. What a pile of shite that one turned out to be.'

'So, I presume our Lieutenant Samson has got us into something rather shitty?' asked Meadows again.

'The silly little school boy has done that, for sure,' replied McGrew. 'I wish I could tell the stupid little toff to wind his bloody neck in. Too much upper-crust English gun-ho about the lad. No offence meant about the "English" aspect.'

Meadows grinned. 'None taken, Serge. Oh shit! I bet the troop's going down the hill and over the stream into the open fields yonder, where all those nice woods are along the river. Where Jerry'll be hiding in his big "bugger off" tanks and bigger "chew on this" eighty-eights, waiting for silly Tommy to come trotting along on a scouting mission. Is that it, Serge? Into that little buffer zone?'

'You are always the mystic clairvoyant, aren't you now, Meadows? That's exactly what our Lieutenant Samson volunteered us for. A quick scouting patrol down and over the stream, into the next meadow beyond, where there's a sizeable wooded area that'll have no Jerry lurking and waiting. You see, our troop commander thinks Jerry forgot such cover and won't be waiting for silly old Tommy like us to come trotting along, singing "Polly-wolly-doodle all the blooming day". The observation group reported no movement across the stream but went on to insist over the radio that Jerry was probably well concealed, anyway. I mean, the type of Jerry we're facing is not likely to show his position. And Jerry'll be aware that us lot are watching. They aren't likely to help us out by throwing a blooming party, that's for sure.'

Meadows sighed. 'Which means the observation group thinks Jerry's still there and we get to be the Mr Glums that are on our way? That's the trouble with these young officers. They seem to think it's a test run around some racetrack, then a trot back home for a rub down with the *Sporting Life* and a nice mention in a dispatch box somewhere or other. Samson must really want to earn his colourful ribbon by the sound of it all.'

'We are due to go in just over an hour from now. I got O'Hara and Louis preparing a few things inside little Molly mare. I haven't told them anything yet, but they have probably put two and two together. They're good troopers. We all are, and I want to get us through this shitshow. We've come too far to fall at the final hurdle.'

'We'll scout on, Serge. We always do and, let's be honest, we've come through some tight spots along the way. We're going to have to be sharp on this little outing.'

McGrew nodded in agreement, but it was with a speculative reminiscence. 'Each ordeal seems to take good troopers from us on this bloody journey. It seems to have been a slow but consistent thing. Ever since we lost young Harry Edwards at the start, back in Libya. Then there was that next time in Tunisia when we lost Caterpillar. A whole host of good lads, coming and going along the way. One after another. And I've got a dreadful feeling about Wingnut.'

Meadows nodded and muttered, 'Good old Caterpillar Miller. Another poor sod. I thought he was alright. He got out of the tank with me. It was you I thought was gone. It was the second time I pulled you from a burning tank, a matter of lightning striking twice. Caterpillar and I had our attention fixed on you. I remember he was talking to me as I was pulling you away from that burning Yank job, the second hit we suffered. That Sturmgeschütz with its little fat barrel. What was we in? A Lee or a Grant?'

'I'm not sure now, but I think it was a Lee. Both tanks look similar and we never had it that long,' McGrew answered. 'I just remember coming to and seeing my bloody feet at ten to two again. They were being dragged across the stony ground and the tank was burning. I thought I was re-living that episode with the Italian field gun, except there was no screaming on that occasion, thanks be to God. Caterpillar wasn't inside burning to death. Everyone got out. Louis, O'Hara and Impett had got out and were on the other side of the burning tank. I was—'

Meadows jumped in and said, 'Muttering, "Déjà vu, déjà vu." I never knew what it meant until you told me afterwards. The French do have some good words for things. Words that become universal.'

'It was a horrid form of déjà vu,' added McGrew as he pondered – reflecting on a deep and hidden remorse, a regret for the loss of so many of his troopers. 'My God! We've seen our fair share of mates go, isn't that for sure, John? All good fellas taken before their prime. I have an overwhelming desire to see them all again. I'm certain I shall, one day.'

'You have a strong faith in God, Serge. I wish I did,' said Meadows, sighing.

'I do, John. I would know of our good men again,' McGrew replied.

Meadows sighed again. 'Perhaps it's not always good to dwell on these things, Serge. I try to shut them out. I don't like going back there, especially young Edwards, when all this sorrow really began. It's been a bastard journey through this shitshow. And now, the finish line is in sight.'

'On the contrary, John. I think I need to feel the hurt of these departed mates. Good men that I would sooner touch through the hurt of their loss as opposed to forgetting about them. I can't help that, you see. I can't get over how Caterpillar was chatting and helping me and then he just sat down on the sand and died beside us as we watched that burning tank. He was mortally injured, but he hid it. He was trying to help me. The man never said a word. He was all smiles helping us out of the burning tank, walking beside us as you dragged me away from yet another burning tank. The second of three – two down and one more to go at that time.'

'I reckon I can understand the way you view things, Serge, but sometimes I can't help feeling you blame yourself.'

'No, John.' McGrew often called Meadows by his first name when discussing the past during light moments of their battle recollections. 'I know it is, what it is. There is nothing we can do to change it. I just like to reassure myself now and then when I'm immersed in heartfelt hurt. I tell myself, that somewhere, out there in eternity, there has to be a kindly alcove where we can all be in that truck on that fine day. When we were all laughing and happy. Little Harry Edwards will be singing "Polly-wolly-doodle all the day".'

'That one works for me.' Meadows smiled. 'I can imagine that. All of us bouncing up and down, ribbing one another and singing along. All of us crammed into that truck. They're probably waiting for us, Serge, with a crate of beers, we must hope.'

'Oh, definitely with beers and perhaps a drop of mellow Irish whiskey too. Or is that pushing it too far?' asked McGrew humorously. He had come through the melancholy stage in the spirited way he always seemed to do.

'I reckon the Almighty would throw in a good bottle of Irish for you, Serge.'

'That's most kind of the fella.' McGrew laughed. 'Now back to another matter. How is our young recruit Wingnut coming along in your opinion? Do you get the same old bad vibes the way we did with the others?'

'I do, Serge. I know it's all superstition, but I do worry about our Wingnut. He looks like another poor little sod who won't make the whole show. I hope I'm wrong, but I just feel that way. I like the bloke, he's a sound fella, but the others were too.'

'That sounds like the kiss of death, John Meadows. You're a real bag of laughs, that's for sure.'

'As I say, Serge, I honestly hope I'm wrong. He's a decent lad. I like him and I think Louis and O'Hara do too. But, as we know, that's the jinx of the trouble. We must never grow to like them, but how can we not help liking Wingnut? The lad's another good 'un.'

'Well, I would ask you to let him know about our little reconnaissance mission that's coming. I sent him to get some provisions and he'll be back soon. I'm going to see how Louis and O'Hara are getting on.'

'Will do, Serge,' agreed Meadows. 'I'll go find the lad and give him a hand back with those provisions.'

McGrew grinned as he left Meadows to find Wingnut. The seasoned sergeant walked off to the vicinity he knew his Cromwell tank would be. Along the way, he passed other tanks parked within the fringe of the woods. He recognised troopers from Canada and Poland but was aware there would be other Allied nations beside the British forces. Most of the troopers idled and chatted with infantrymen or worked about their tanks, not just Cromwell tanks, but other models similar to Churchills and even one odd Achilles. There was also a large number of acquired American Sherman tanks. They were deeper in the woods.

'The good old lend-lease programme,' muttered McGrew in satisfaction. 'Where would we be without it?'

His morale was lifted again by the sight of Staff Sharky's impressive Firefly support tank – a splendid adaptation of the American M4 Sherman. British and Commonwealth forces had removed the American gun and replaced it with a longer-barrelled British artillery gun – the Ordnance Quick-Firing seventeen-pounder anti-tank gun. The Achilles he had passed also had such an anti-tank gun, but he hadn't paid much attention to it. A Sherman Firefly and or an Achilles tank destroyer would often support a platoon on reconnaissance.

The sergeant searched among the various armoured vehicles for his unit's little Molly mare. His pace had slowed for he knew Molly would be in close proximity to Staff Sharky's Firefly. His mood lifted. He spotted the small form of Trooper Billy O'Hara. There was the unit's brash rascal standing at the front of their much-loved tank – their live-in mechanical steel-clad steed. The loveable nag on tracks. The iron beast's dark green metal was splattered and smeared by rain and mud. Sloppy insignia and other markings grinned through the cloudy muck – the diminished white markings seemed to enhance every muddy footprint and weathered patch, especially the rain streaks running down from the rivets. Various tools and rolled coverings were tied and clamped about the vehicle. The front of the long gun barrel was blackened from the discharge of past shells, especially in recent encounters since the Ardennes conflict. Some of the other tanks had a lacklustre winter-white paint. McGrew and his crew hadn't done so with Molly. They hadn't been given any such order and McGrew couldn't see the point. The snow would be gone soon – most of it had already thawed.

Beyond such weathered blemishes, the crew had a fondness for Molly the Cromwell tank, more so than for the past tanks that had been allocated to them. Molly could move quicker than anything they had used before and there was a strange comfort in such knowledge.

McGrew stopped beside O'Hara. The trooper was leaning on the front of the vehicle talking through the open circular driver's hatch. Louis was looking out, showing off his beaming white teeth in a fixed smile.

'Is it clear now?' asked O'Hara. He had been cleaning the lens of the driver's periscope with a wet rag.

Louis called back in his squeaky cockney accent, 'Yep, that looks good. How's things, Serge?'

O'Hara looked behind and was pleasantly surprised to see McGrew. 'I never noticed yer there, that's for sure.'

'Things are good here and there. Things are also bad, here and there,' McGrew answered flippantly. 'But I would want to be sticking with the good things for the time being. What about you, lads? How's it all with Molly? Our gorgeous little nag is in fine shape, I hope?'

'All the necessary shells and bullets for all the guns are stored and ready, Serge,' said O'Hara, grinning with delight.

'Now, that is a bonny thing to know. Good on that score then, Billy O'Hara. I'm glad everything is in order?'

Louis called out through the circular driver's hatchway and added, 'Molly's running like a dream, Serge. If she was a real girl, I would try to chat her up.'

'Now isn't that good to know too, Louis. I'm betting Molly would have a drink and a dance with you, if she were a real girl. Unfortunately, she's our nifty little iron pony,' said McGrew as he clambered onto the hull and further up onto the turret. He dropped nimbly down into the tank via the open cupola hatch and onto the cramped turret platform. He was careful to watch for the gun loader's seat and that of the gunner's too, a lesson he had learned the hard way. He pulled his commander's seat down, something he could do when the cupola doors were open. The entire area was very cramped and with Meadows and Wingnut in position, the turret space would be even more restricted.

His nostrils flared and he was gladdened to realise that the smell of fuel was not so strong – something he often noticed when Molly was dormant with many of the hatches open. He could tell Louis had been running the Merlin engine, but it was switched off now. Then he happily looked forward beyond the gun's breech to resume his small talk with Louis, sitting in his driver compartment.

'I bet our Molly would be a timid Coleen, that's for sure. Not aware of just how lovely a young lady she really is.'

'What, Serge, one of those little shy fillies that stands in the corner of the dance hall with a group of other less confident and equally shy girlfriends?' asked Louis, chuckling at the metaphorical vision.

'The very type,' replied McGrew with a smile.

O'Hara opened the auxiliary gunner's hull access door. It was a small side panel with an upper plate cover that he pulled outwards. He climbed into his section and sat next to Louis and pulled the small door shut. Quickly, he ran through more methodical checks of his front machine gun. He knew the routine off by heart and all appeared well. He looked behind him and noticed Sergeant McGrew inspecting the breech mechanism and the gunner's telescope. Then the tank commander began to scrutinise his commander's periscope and was nodding in a satisfactory manner. All of a sudden, he tutted and stopped. For a moment, Louis and O'Hara thought McGrew had found something wrong. Alas no, McGrew turned and raised his commander's seat back up against the turret's plate.

'The bloody thing gets in the way. It's always digging in my back, so it is. And I have a wee phobia about sticking my big head out of the turret when we're on the move, that's for sure.'

'Oh, aye – we've noticed that. Though it's with good reason, Serge,' said O'Hara in a good-humoured tone.

'Yep,' agreed Louis. 'Especially after what happened to Lieutenant Nightingale.'

McGrew continued to check his commander's periscope, muttering, 'I'm afraid the lieutenant was a young lad that wouldn't be told. Now we have Lieutenant Samson. Another one who won't be told.'

'They need to learn the on-the-job things. Sometimes there's not enough time,' added Louis.

'I can't understand them sticking their heads out of the cupola when we're entering enemy territory. Especially here. The amount of men we've lost so far! All for stopping bullets with their heads!' added O'Hara.

'Jerry must think it's open season on Tommy,' said Louis.

'For a time, I thought it was a bloody turkey shoot back in France. Jerry must have thought Brit officers were rabid and wanted to commit suicide,' added O'Hara. 'That sniper we caught thought so.'

'You were going to shoot him,' said Louis, reminiscing.

'Lots of units shoot snipers. Jerry does too,' added O'Hara. He turned to look at McGrew like a little urchin that had been denied his pudding.

'We don't shoot Jerry when he has surrendered, Billy. If I had a shilling for each time I stopped you shooting a captured Jerry, I'd have a few bob by now. When Jerry has surrendered, that's it – take him prisoner and pass the poor sod on. They are just trying to survive the shitshow. The way the rest of us are,' McGrew said, his manner becoming a little testy while he continued to check his periscope.

'You never know,' said Louis, 'one day a grateful Jerry prisoner might do a good turn for you, Billy.'

McGrew nodded his agreement. He wanted to change the subject, and finished his scrutiny of the commander's periscope. 'All looks good, boys. It won't be long now before Meadows and Wingnut are with us. Maybe we'll see the new lad's gunnery in action. The rookie's being thrown in at the deep end, but Lieutenant Samson says he had some good marks for gunnery before he came to us. As you may well have guessed, we are about to go out on a scouting mission. A little canter across the meadow, beyond the stream at the bottom of the field and into the fields on the other side. There's a gentle rise and we're to go up there and take a look beyond.'

'Do you mean over the little stream that flows into the main river, Serge?' asked O'Hara.

'The very one,' replied McGrew.

'Over the bleeding hills and far away,' added Louis. 'I do hope they've considered that stretch of woodland along the river's bank. It'll be on our left flank as we go on this jolly jaunt. Once we cross that little stream that flows into the river, I reckon the fun will start.'

'Oh, aye. If you're a Jerry,' added O'Hara flippantly.

Louis ignored the pessimistic remark, even though he knew O'Hara was right. 'The stream becomes a pretty little waterfall, I'm told.'

O'Hara chuckled. 'It's not a waterfall as such. More of a water trickle. Any of us pissing into the river would make a better water trickle than that stream does.'

McGrew tried to make them feel at ease. 'Well, the wooded area on this side of the stream has had an observation unit on our side of the slope. They're hidden in a huge thicket of overhanging holly, so I've been told. They've been watching for over twenty-four hours.'

'Are they the unit that never saw the Sturmgeschütz roll up the hill and go past? The Sturmgeschütz that the Poles walloped?' O'Hara was not inspired by the knowledge of an observation unit.

'Is this observation unit on our side of the little stream?' Louis wanted to be sure.

McGrew nodded affirmatively and added, 'Yes, Louis. Close to the small copse of trees on our side, by the steep drop to the river. This observation unit are in a well-camouflaged and concealed position. They have been watching for almost twenty-four hours and have radioed no movement or sign of Jerry activity.'

O'Hara was not impressed. 'But that there Sturmgeschütz came up via the scarp at that location. The observer unit didn't see them or hear them. That means, just because they can't see or hear something, it might still be there.'

McGrew grinned. 'Just because Billy "Boy" O'Hara knows he's mistrustful, it doesn't mean people should be trusted.' He laughed a little more.

'Well, that doesn't inspire confidence, Serge. Let's be honest. How the heck does a great big "bugger off" tank waltz up that incline and pass an observer unit without getting ruddy noticed?' O'Hara was looking very concerned.

'Well,' began McGrew, 'that was sure one hell of a bombardment during the night. It was loud and blustery winds too. The observer unit may have kept their heads down during that and if the Sturmgeschütz clung to the slight drop along the edge when passing the small copse, no one would hear or see it. I thought Jerry was stupid taking their assault gun up alongside the upper woods where we are. They must have known we were firing from that position. What was on the minds of the Jerry crew?'

Louis removed his glasses to clean them again and then added, 'HQ must be suspicious of the wooded area along this side, especially further along the river beyond the connecting stream. It's very noticeable that all of our traffic is crossing the pontoon bridge and nothing is moving along the road running parallel with the opposite bank. A good hiding place for a Sturmgeschütz or their eighty-eight flak guns to fire from. None of our vehicles are using that section of the road.'

McGrew sighed. 'I agree, Louis. That's why they are crossing the pontoon bridge and not staying on the road as it runs past the trees on the opposite bank. We've seen this sort of thing before. I get what you're implying and the dangers the woodland presents. Staff Sharky mentioned it during the briefing. According to the reports from the observation crew down by the copse on our side of the stream, there's been no movement at all.'

'Do we know who the observation unit are?' O'Hara enquired.

'Davis and his troopers,' answered McGrew.

'Well, that's something, I suppose. Not much escapes that little crew. They are good,' added Louis.

'Oh aye, we'll not mention a great big "bugger off" Sturmgeschütz.' O'Hara wasn't going to let up on the issue.

'To be fair, Davis reckons he's seen nothing,' answered McGrew, 'but according to Staff Sharky, Davis thinks there must be something because the position is too good for Jerry not to use. He said Jerry would probably be experienced and well-camouflaged and concealed just the way Davis' observation lads are. Even though we've put many shells into the wood, the observation unit think Jerry is still there.'

'Bloody hell,' muttered Louis. 'Not exactly a party atmosphere, then?'

'Aye,' agreed O'Hara, nodding his support. 'How far and how long is this little scout about going to be?'

'Not too far, I hope,' replied McGrew, trying to seem light-hearted. But in essence he was not, and no doubt Louis and O'Hara knew this.

'Will we have an Achilles or a Firefly with the troop, Serge?' asked Louis.

'We do have the comfort of a seventeen-pounder seconded to help us – a Firefly, I've been told by Lieutenant Samson. He will be troop commander in Jenny with me as the second troop commander, and Corporal Chandler as commander of Mildred. I'm sure you have already guessed that the Firefly aiding us is commanded by Staff Sergeant Sharky. So, I'm sure that little snippet of news will be a little reassuring to you.'

There followed a murmur of approval from Louis and a pleasing nod from O'Hara. The Firefly crew were highly regarded.

'I'm sure Staff Sharky will do for you lads, that's for sure.' McGrew grinned at his two troopers. 'We'll have a little time before Lieutenant Samson gives us the word to proceed.'

'Any idea how long, Serge?' asked Louis.

'We are scheduled to move at 14.15. Another hour to go yet, lads,' replied McGrew as he checked the three-tier radio. He switched between IC then to A and then B on his microphone intercom – nothing could be left out.

'I can't see Staff Sharky being over the moon about that woodland being on our flank,' Louis said.

'Well, Staff Sharky is very uncomfortable about it, that's for sure, Louis. But his crew are coming anyway.' McGrew took out a pack of cigarettes. He put one in his mouth and offered Louis and O'Hara the pack.

'I always get that same old eerie feeling just before we set off,' said O'Hara. 'Once we get moving then I feel better. It's just the blooming waiting. Especially for a scout about like this. I know Jerry is done for, but sometimes I think they still don't realise it yet. They don't give up easily, that's for sure.'

McGrew nodded. 'I think they must know the writing's on the wall. They're desperate. I think their bigwigs must know there will be a reckoning when the shitshow is over. There'll be a lot of judgemental people coming for them. Look at some of the things we've come across. There must be some sort of reckoning?'

'Oh, aye. All those Jerry bigwigs still sitting behind their desks will know they have their cards marked. They will have to atone for this shitshow, that's for sure.' O'Hara smiled with his usual comical grin, showing a noticeable gummy gap where his front teeth used to be.

McGrew added, 'I know, lads. Jerry still has plenty of fight left in him and the final few furlongs are going to be as tough as anything we've been through, that's for sure.'

Louis tutted and shook his head. He wished the Irishmen would stop finishing every sentence with 'that's for sure'. 'I thought we'd got through the crueller aspects of fighting in North Africa with Edwards' horrible death and then I saw those human torches jumping out that burning Italian M13. I was wrong about that. It was a baptism for more dreadful things to come. Now I sometimes think I've become numb to it all.'

'I thought Italy was terrible at times,' added O'Hara. 'I thought it couldn't get any worse after that.'

McGrew sighed. 'And then along comes D-Day to here and now. The entire shitshow just seems to pull off bigger and more repulsive horrors every step of the way. It must surely end soon. Nothing goes on forever.'

'I wouldn't hold your breath, Serge,' said Louis.

For a while, an uneasy silence fell upon the crew. It was as though each man wanted to indulge in small talk but there was a lack of topics to speak about. It always came back around to the dreadful aspects of the war.

O'Hara decided to break the tense silence that was beginning to make them all feel uncomfortable. 'What do you think of our new boy, Serge? Does Wingnut have what it takes?'

McGrew sighed. 'All of the poor sods had what it takes, now, O'Hara. Every one of them, that's for sure. The question is whether our Wingnut is a survivor like us four have been, thus far.'

'Thus far, being the *definitely maybe* word, Serge,' replied Louis.

'Indeed, it is, Louis. How can we gauge, *definitely maybe?*' McGrew started to chuckle. 'I like that decisively indecisive couple of words.'

O'Hara's eyes narrowed as though he was puzzled. 'I sense that means there's an issue, Serge? Are we having morbid premonitions for our Wingnut lad? Surely not. Not like the others?'

Louis sighed. 'Molly needs her five-man crew. Therefore, five must make it to the finish line. One of them will be a rookie.'

O'Hara looked at Louis. 'Are we assuming that us four veterans of the desert and Italy are going to see the whole show?'

McGrew raised an eyebrow. 'To be fair, lads, there's always an issue with a new recruit. We've seen a number come and go. I just don't like dwelling on such things. Each time one of them falls, it's like another slice of yer soul is hacked away.'

'And you suspect it will happen again?' replied Louis. 'Before the shitshow is over?'

'I can't see young Wingnut being any different,' McGrew answered. 'He seems a fine trooper with a good strong sense of responsibility. Dependable too, but then the others were like that as well. Such attributes didn't save those poor sods, in the long run.'

Louis sighed. 'What does Meadows make of the lad? Does he think Wingnut has the makings of another poor sod?'

'Aye.' O'Hara nodded approvingly. 'We do rely on Meadows' outlook. He always seems to get it right.'

'Perhaps we are all getting a little too superstitious and I'm not always sure we should believe in our own continued luck,' said McGrew. He was frowning while he scrutinised one of the turret revolver ports.

O'Hara had finished re-examining the Besa machine gun and continued with further inspections around his front gunner compartment. He twisted about in his seat to inspect the electrically operated extraction fan.

'You know, Serge,' continued O'Hara as he went about his system checks, 'we do seem to have become incredibly superstitious. Meadows is like the magic witch doctor. We tend to put a lot of faith in his speculations.'

'I know,' agreed McGrew. 'He does tend to get this vibe about things, like he knows what's coming. He seems to think we are always going to be the survivors and the newcomers are always here for a short time.'

'So far, his predictions have been right. Does he get the same sad vibes about this Wingnut lad, then? Is he insistent? Meadows is like the kiss of death with his bad omens. A few hundred years back, he would have been tied to a stake and burned. He wouldn't have reached twenty,' Louis mumbled with a smouldering Woodbine cigarette hanging from his lips. He was gently running his hand around the rota-trailer hook control and then down to his right-hand side where the engine controls were. A little feel around the accelerator hand lever, then on to the carburettor strangler lever. He was also mentally building himself up – the tension of waiting for the word to go. It was always like this. Every time. The three of them were beginning to feel the pressure. When they moved off, there would be some release, but while they waited, the best thing they could do was talk. Even if it was feeble small talk.

'Our fortunes during this shitshow have been strange. Meadows says we have an aurora around us,' added O'Hara.

'What the heck is an aurora?' asked McGrew, giggling and coughing on his cigarette.

'That sounds like a made-up Meadows word,' added Louis who was laughing too. He'd had the good sense to take his cigarette out of his mouth.

O'Hara gave them a big toothless grin. 'It's something that shines and dazzles – a bit like your big sparkling teeth. Something to do with the Northern Lights in the sky. A magical shine of sorts.'

Louis went into full-blown, high-pitched laughter. Laughter that was infectious. Within seconds,

McGrew was laughing too and then finally O'Hara joined in.

'Oh well, how we all blooming roared,' added O'Hara sarcastically. It was a saying he'd heard Wingnut say and he liked it.

It just served to further inflame the high-pitched and uncontrollable laughter. McGrew and Louis had tears coming from their eyes.

'I'm so pleased to have amused my "buddies" as our Yank friends might say.' O'Hara was now laughing along with them as the contagious glee claimed him too and the three of them giggled uncontrollably.

'So, it's a Yank word, then?' asked Louis between chuckles.

'No,' replied O'Hara. 'It's a Meadows word. But then I heard Meadows say aurora is a word that Icelanders use.'

'Oh, Lord love us. So, our Meadows reckons Wingnut doesn't have this aurora?' McGrew was still shaking his head while giggling in disbelief.

'No, our Wingnut hasn't,' replied O'Hara. 'Just bloody big ears.'

Louis was still trying to talk between the laughter. 'Do you know that Merlin engine in the back is used in Spitfires? With Wingnut sticking his head up through the cupola and the speed of the Cromwell tank we could blinking take off. Wingnut would have some aurora around him then. He would be higher than Magic Meadows and his mystic predictions.'

'He takes no notice of it all,' said McGrew. 'From day one his real name has never been used and he has compliantly responded to the nickname Wingnut. No complaint, no anger. As calm as you please. Plain acceptance.'

'He struts around with that dour look, yet without a single care for his nickname,' agreed O'Hara. 'The lad's got some arsehole, that's for sure.'

'Yet our Meadows says he's still a marked man, which is a pity. I've got to like him,' added McGrew. 'That's always a bad sign. I tried to keep the lad at arm's length and to dislike him with those huge great wings for ears. I thought if I could resent the gobshite, he'll stand a chance. After all, I liked all the other ones and looked what happened to them.'

'You can't change the goalposts like that, Serge,' replied Louis. 'What will be will be.'

Gradually the merriment subsided and the amused men continued smoking their Woodbines. The quietness kicked in and it wouldn't be long before the nervous waiting game started again.

'I know something we could do,' said O'Hara.

'What might that be?' replied McGrew.

'That home-made flare gun you attached to the rear of the turret. It's hanging next to our water canisters. You said it would be better taken off and fired from inside without having to stick your head out to use it.' Again, O'Hara displayed his toothless grin.

'Indeed, we did. That's the trouble with our little home-made adaptations. We don't put them on the normal check list and they get overlooked on the normal schedule because they're not on there. Let's sort that one out while we're waiting,' McGrew responded as he got up to climb through the cupola while Louis opened his driver's hatch.

CHAPTER 4

THE SCOUTING PATROL GET READY

'Bloody hell, Wingnut, you got a few things here. Tins of corned beef, more tea and some more packs of cigarettes,' said Meadows as he took a small box of tea, a can of powdered milk and a bag of sugar. The day was still cold but not as biting as a few hours ago when they were looking at the destroyed enemy Sturmgeschütz. Both troopers were making their way back to the tank after collecting the surprise allocation of supplies.

Wingnut grinned. 'I think the sergeant has got a little scout around in the pipeline. Why else would he suddenly need these things? I was told to remind the bloke at the stores about a special favour he owed Sergeant McGrew. Something a bit hush-hush. That was when they gave me the bag of sugar and these cinnamon buns, plus a bag of biscuits.

The nice Dutch people in the last village gave us loads of cakes and biscuits and I think our sergeant had a little finger in the pie.'

'Well, that's a nice little turn up for us. Sergeant McGrew has fingers in lots of pies. I hope Jerry doesn't blow the heck out of us before we get time to eat these dainty little delicacies. They'll be stored outside in the Jerry box.' Meadows had a big beaming smile on his face.

'Do you reckon we're going on a scouting patrol?' asked Wingnut.

'Of course, we're off on a little canter across the fields. Molly needs the ride. You can't keep a good old mare like that stabled for long periods of time. A canter across the fields is well and truly in order. Our new lieutenant got us volunteered up for it all. According to the sergeant, our new "top-ho Charlie" is looking for medals and mentions.'

'Mentions?' asked Wingnut, looking bemused.

'As in, mentions in dispatches. It's a big thing among the big nobs,' added Meadows.

'Oh, I see,' Wingnut nodded, 'and we're the chaps to get him his mentions?'

'That's the size of it. Our Molly mare and the other nags of the platoon are going to be sprats instead of horses.' Meadows sounded glum.

Wingnut was getting more irritated by the traditional jargon. 'I know we were once a cavalry unit back in the day, but do you not think it's taking things a little too far with all this cavalry bollocks. Molly is a tank made of iron, a mechanical vehicle, not a bleeding horse. Why must we keep up the horse stuff all the time?'

'Wash your bleeding mouth out, Wingnut.' Meadows looked disgusted and insulted. 'Molly is our loveable gee-gee. In my humble opinion, the best little mare we've ever had, even if she is made of iron and runs on wheels and tracks. She's a dapper little mare, that's for sure.'

'You did it again,' said Wingnut delightedly. 'You got a touch of the old O'Hara. You just said, "that's for sure".'

'Slip of the tongue, that's all.' Meadows was struggling to defend himself. 'Besides, the sergeant says it too.'

'Yes,' added Wingnut, 'but he's an Ulsterman too.'

'It's the adopted tank talk of our crew. All Molly troopers say such things now. Besides, we were talking about nags. Stick to the point, Wingnut. The subject you chose to harp on about is nags.'

'Why can't we rumble down the field and drive through the silly shallow stream and then rev up into the next field on the opposite bank? I'm presuming that is the direction we're going in.'

'Because, Wingnut, me old fruit, Molly will canter off down the field, jump the stream and gallop up the field on the other side. That's what this troop does on a scouting patrol, me old mucker, even in our big "bugger off" tank. Christ! You are a right nightmare geezer, Wingnut. Come on in, the water's lovely. I bet the mice sling themselves onto the mouse traps when you walk through your mum's front door.'

Wingnut's face retained the unamused dour look, while his pronounced ears stuck out sideways beneath his neat black beret. 'You lads have a colourful way with words, in more ways than one. I think the Molly crew have a ruddy language all of their own.'

'Every tank crew does. I bet Jerry tank crews have their jargon too,' replied Meadows with an air of confidence.

'I suppose this is so. But I find it hard to visualise Jerry with a sense of humour.' Wingnut had watched many newsreels of the enemy leader speaking into a microphone in a strange language that was lost to him. 'Hitler always seems to be shouting and hollering. He always looks like a ruddy angry bloke to me.'

'Well, I'm sure our Adolf has his light-hearted moments,' replied Meadows. 'He is a rather snappy dresser, you have to give the geezer that.'

Wingnut was appalled but retained his usual bland and emotionless look. 'There is nothing good about that madman. How can you say things like that?'

Meadows chuckled. 'Touched a sore spot, have I? How do you do that without any facial expression. Your words sound cross, yet you look matter-of-fact.'

'Well, I'm not one to create a scene. I may as well just calmly ask.' Wingnut was matter-of-fact again as he held his cardboard tray of buns and other assorted sweet things.

'You know, Wingnut. You really do baffle me. I think they broke the mould when you were conceived. How do you keep this dry and rather bland attitude? Even when you're flustered by something, it doesn't appear to faze you. What goes on behind those bulbous eyeballs of yours?'

'I thought you might have said, "between your ears". Let's face it, they are a topic of general conversation,' added Wingnut in his same dry manner.

'Sometimes I'm not sure how to make you out,' said Meadows, laughing.

'What are you trying to work out?' asked Wingnut in his dismal tone.

'Whether you want to crap or get a haircut.' Meadows sniggered.

'Oh, how we roared,' Wingnut replied in his dreary manner.

'You never complain about your nickname either. Why is that?'

Wingnut actually stopped walking for a few seconds. He may have been stunned by the question but it didn't show on his impassive face. 'I do not believe for one moment it would stop the troop saying it. Back at the barracks the RSM told me to get used to it.'

'So, they called you Wingnut back at the training ground too.' Meadows chuckled.

'They did start to call me by my Christian name just before I left. I thought it might have been a show of respect. However, that little hope was soon washed away. My real name, as you know, is Leslie McGurk.'

'Are you a cardboard Paddy like Louis and me then? Ones that have never been to the Emerald Isle in their entire life?'

'I'm English,' replied Wingnut. 'Plenty of English have Irish surnames. Louis is a black man. I didn't think there were many black men in Ireland.'

'Louis Donnell's mother is white. His dad was from the West Indies. Jamaica, I think. He died before Louis was born.'

'Was his dad a sailor that met his mother when he was docked in London?'

'Yeah,' replied Meadows. 'How did you know that?'

'Just an educated guess. There are a lot of people with Irish surnames. Is that why they put me in an Irish cavalry regiment? At the training ground there were a number of Irish lads but most of the English had some form of Irish descent.'

'Yeah, I know. A lot of English people have Irish surnames,' added Meadows. 'Probably something to do with the famine. My old nan often went on about it. As to why there are us English in an Irish regiment, I don't know the politics of that situation. But, let's be honest, a large number of English have Irish, Scots or Welsh somewhere along the ancestral tree. Does it matter?'

'Your name – Meadows sounds very English to me,' added Wingnut.

'It is English – completely and utterly Anglo-Saxon. My father's people are English through and through. They were all from Suffolk to my knowledge. I only have a grandmother who's Irish on my mother's side. I'm English, mate, and my English surname sounds like the name of a butler – a name belonging to someone—'

'Out of a P.G. Wodehouse novel?' Wingnut finished.

Meadows looked impressed. 'How did you know I was going to say that? About a butler?'

'I like P.G. Wodehouse and I've read the Mr Mulliner stories on occasion. Especially the "Archibald and the Masses" story. His valet is called Meadows – it's all very hoity-toity upper-crust English.'

Meadows looked directly into Wingnut's face. He wanted to see a smile or something with a hint of humour. But it was void. Totally expressionless. Not a hint of emotion or feeling anywhere.

'You're a bleeding wind-up merchant, aren't you? The bloody deadpan man. That's what you are, Wingnut, a chap loaded with dry wit. You're a deliberate display of emotional neutrality. How can you do that without your face even showing a crease of amusement?' Meadows was impressed. 'You got something with that face, especially if you could plug a good inuendo-style joke.'

'While everyone else gets to roar?' replied Wingnut, looking down at his tray of buns as he ambled along. 'Oh, how they would roar.'

Meadows nodded with a look of revelation. 'O'Hara just started saying that. He got that from you, didn't he?'

'Well, here's Molly,' said Wingnut, which was a subtle way of asking Meadows to stop going on. Sergeant McGrew had just climbed out of the cupola while Louis had emerged from the driver's hatch.

'Yep, here we are. Let's get aboard the old nag then,' said Meadows, trying to get a reaction. 'Just for the last page, why was you disappointed when the training ground started calling you by your real name?'

'They just called me Les, but then added miserable as in the French novel, *Les Misérables* by Victor Hugo. I happened to be reading it at the time.'

Once again Meadows chuckled as he climbed up onto the hull. McGrew and Louis were dismantling their bodged smoke grenade gun that was crudely fixed to the turret. They seemed oblivious to the arrival of Meadows and Wingnut.

'All bets are on with our Wingnut or Les Miserable. Take your pick.' Meadows laughed. 'That was his nickname as well, you know.'

'Too long-winded,' muttered Louis, watching over McGrew's fiddling with the smoke grenade launcher. 'Wingnut sounds better.'

O'Hara's hull gunner door swung out and he popped up with a big toothless grin on his face. 'I'll store them for you, lads, that's for sure.'

'Only take a few things, Billy,' called McGrew. 'The rest can go in the Jerry box.'

'Can I take the sugar?' he called back. 'We'll need the sugar.'

'Just the sugar then,' replied McGrew.

'We'll need the tea and the powdered milk too,' added O'Hara, looking at Meadows.

Meadows took a step back and stood beside Wingnut to give the gunner his items. 'So, you want everything I'm carrying inside Molly?'

'Very well,' answered Sergeant McGrew. 'The sugar, the tea, and the powdered milk can go in the tank. The rest is for the Jerry box.'

'And a bun?' O'Hara called back, deciding to push his luck.

'Yeah,' Meadows agreed. 'Just one little cinnamon bun, Serge? Can't be no harm in that?'

'If you must.' McGrew laughed.

'So, we can each have a bun?' Meadows' face lit up.

'Just one each and then put the rest in the Jerry box,' agreed McGrew, smiling. 'Yer all like a load of kids wanting to devour the goodies straight away, so yer are.'

Wingnut waited as O'Hara selected a bun. He looked to Meadows who took one, and then he stood before Sergeant McGrew and Trooper Louis – both were still fiddling with the flare gun fixings on the turret. McGrew and Louis each selected a bun with gratitude. Then McGrew nodded to the back of the tank where the stowage was fastened, with ropes holding down all sorts of boxes and folded bivouacs. There were also a number of clamped-down tools. 'The Jerry box is the big one among the stowage ropes. It's got the Nazi emblem stamped on the front – we salvaged it back at Caen. Put the rest in there please, Wingnut. Oh, and take a bun for yourself.'

Meadows was waiting for someone to take his remaining items. 'I have some fag packs and tobacco pouches. What about them?'

'Put them in the Jerry box too,' replied McGrew. 'We still have a good stash with us at the moment.'

'That's an awful lot of rummy stuff on the stowage, Serge,' replied Meadows. 'Are you sure you don't want any more inside Molly?'

'No!' snapped McGrew. 'For the love of God, it's cramped enough inside, John. We need the room.'

Wingnut stepped over to the stowage at the rear of Molly. The Jerry box was the most prominent among all the other boxes and rolled materials.

'The ropes are very tight. Do you want me to undo them?'

'No!' came the panicked response from the entire tank crew.

'Blimey! Keep your hair on. I was just asking.' Wingnut's face remained expressionless, despite the remark.

Meadows chuckled. 'Pardon our enthusiasm, Wingnut. But we have cunning little doors in our Jerry box, craftily fashioned so we don't have to undo the said tethering. They're nice and tight for our stowage and we wants to keep them that way, me old mucker.'

'One of your tickety-boo smooth order of things?' Wingnut asked.

'It's like this, Wingnut,' added Louis, looking up from the dismantled flare gun holder, 'liberators get us these treasured little goodies. In this instance, Sergeant McGrew was the liberator of such fine goods. We have our little ways of stowage outside of

Molly. We only keep a small quantity inside our tank for the odd brew.'

'Oh, I see,' replied Wingnut. 'Makes sense, but the Jerry box and some of the other items have bullet holes in them.'

'Molly is always stopping bullets for us, Wingnut,' answered McGrew.

'Oh aye, that's for sure,' added O'Hara.

'Well, better Molly than one of us, I suppose,' Wingnut replied, nodding his approval at the veterans.

Louis looked back at the smoke gun fixings. 'This is proving a little more aggravating than expected.'

'Checking the smoke grenade gun, I see,' Wingnut said with a polite and enquiring manner. He had found the upper lid on the Jerry box and lifted it open.

'That's right, lad,' replied McGrew. 'I've a feeling we may need them.'

'We're not leaving the thing fixed outside of the vehicle anymore,' added Louis. 'Opening the hatch, then leaning out to fire it, is a bit too risky, especially when there are shells and bullets flying around.'

Wingnut was putting the remaining items away and then scratched the side of his jaw. 'I wondered about it. A little exclusive adaptation of your own making, like you do with the drink canisters. I haven't seen them on other Cromwell tanks.'

'Each crew does their own little things,' said Meadows as he put the cigarette cartons and tobacco pouches inside the Jerry box too.

McGrew added, 'This is one of my little creations. A not too good one. Many crews make their own little constructions, lad. This one turned out to be a load of old crap – fixing a converted flare pistol to the rear of the turret. So, we've reviewed this some more, and now we've decided to keep this wee fella inside Molly with us. I can open the hatch and fire the thing into the air without sticking my head out if we have to make a run for it. The lads are getting a wee bit nervous of me getting my head blown off. It makes me feel all warm and wanted.'

'Do you think we're going to be running from the enemy then?' asked Wingnut.

'We are in the middle of a war,' added O'Hara. 'We do tend to run into the enemy from time to time. Sometimes they have some serious muscle as weapons and stuff goes. Jerry is a tough old sod, that's for sure. Yer Jerry tends to shoot first and ask questions later.'

Wingnut ignored the humorous rebuke and continued to observe Louis in his efforts to disconnect the fixing with the flare gun.

McGrew replied, 'Yes, Wingnut. We will almost assuredly run into Jerry if they are in those ruddy tree clusters on the other side of the stream. I reckon we can let off three smoke flares every fifteen to twenty seconds if we have to make a run for it.'

'A nice big pile of smoke to the rear will be very helpful if we need cover for a hasty retreat,' added Louis.

'Why are we going over there if you think this is going to happen?' Wingnut was genuinely bemused.

McGrew, who was clearly agitated by the platoon's orders, answered, 'Because sometimes we have to dangle a carrot and tempt Jerry out. They'll have to fire on us if we get close to their concealed position. And we will certainly be doing that, young Wingnut. Our top brass doesn't think Jerry has much in the way of hardware. How they arrived at such a conclusion, I don't know. Maybe they've been given some intelligence. I also think our gullible new officer, the dashing Lieutenant Samson, believes this too. He was awful quick to get us on this reconnaissance patrol. We've been through this type of thing before. If they are in the treeline, I'm of the opinion that they'll have the ability to give our tank platoon a run for its money. They'll not be up to the entire force we have up here in the woods, but they can dish it out on a small scouting patrol.'

'Ruddy heck! It sounds like a right party atmosphere,' mumbled Meadows in his usual disapproving manner.

'It won't be the first time we've done something like this,' added Louis.

'Aye,' agreed O'Hara. 'And it won't be the last, that's for sure.'

Wingnut looked out over the basin and across the stream. The woods along the main river were not lost on him and he suspected an enemy presence to be there. He had no combat experience, but he could see the enemy's benefit of the woods against the river and the approach road on the opposite bank.

McGrew decided to try to inspire the young trooper. 'You came to us with some good reports about your gunnery in these particular nags. We'll need you to be focused, lad. Are you up to it? You have the look.'

'I think I am, Serge. I won't let you down, that's for sure,' Wingnut replied with an unusual smile, using the Ulstermen's little saying.

McGrew raised an eyebrow and grinned. 'Humour from our Wingnut.'

'He reads a lot of P.G. Wodehouse too,' added Meadows.

'Does he?' replied Louis. 'Who the blooming heck is P.G. Wodehouse?'

There was a stunned silence for a few seconds. Then slowly all heads turned to Louis in shock horror.

'Have you never seen that flick called *Thank You, Jeeves!*? Arthur Treacher and David Niven?' asked Meadows.

'I know of Jeeves the butler,' answered Louis. 'But I'm not a flicks man like you, Meadows. How often did you go to the pictures when back in Civvy street?'

'Often as I could. As for Jeeves and Wooster, well, Wodehouse writes them,' said Meadows.

'And our Wingnut is fond of reading them?' asked McGrew.

'That's for sure.' Wingnut decided to push his luck.

Another moment of stunned quietness. How dare a fledgling be so cocky? The deadpan and expressionless face just stared back with an impervious air of innocence. It was not real innocence. They had all learned that Wingnut was a dry sod. But there wasn't a signal the rest of the tank crew could pick up on.

'He's a dry sod, alright,' said O'Hara with his toothless gummy grin. He looked to Meadows. 'Knows how to stoke and keep things simmering. Back home, those blooming theatre agents would like him.'

'Spent all your time reading books, did you? Are you a virgin, Wingnut? You look like a lad that hasn't dipped his rod yet,' enquired McGrew, joshing and thinking of young Harry Edwards' comical first encounter with a lady back during the desert war.

Again, Wingnut gave them the same expressionless look and answered, 'Not yet.'

They all made to roar with laughter but gulped and stopped themselves as one. Each was stumped for words – they realised Wingnut was playing them.

O'Hara chuckled from behind. 'Oh, how we did *not* roar.'

'Oh, my word,' said Louis. 'He is one dry little sod, indeed. He has that French, *je ne sais quoi*. I must say, Wingnut, you're very good.'

'Well, I'm sure there is a compliment in there somewhere,' replied Wingnut dryly.

McGrew chuckled and the rest followed suit. Wingnut was a good one. They all appeared to have decided this. In some ways it choked them because they were all immensely superstitious. They had liked so many of their late comrades in the same way. It would be kindly of the Almighty to let just one such lad see the final part of their shitshow out. One likeable recruit, still alive.

'Let's be having you lads inside then,' said McGrew.

Instantly they all got inside Molly through the various service hatches. As McGrew finally dropped down inside, the crew were at their various positions. Louis and O'Hara were back in their seats with Wingnut sitting on the gunner's stall and Meadows by the radio and loader's position. McGrew leaned back against the radio frame while standing on the cramped revolving platform.

'Well, here we are again, lads. All dressed up and ready to go,' said McGrew humorously.

'No decent establishment would let us in wearing these dirty pixie suits,' joked Meadows.

'Do you mind if I ask you blokes a question?' Wingnut was scrutinising Molly's firing mechanism.

'Go on,' said McGrew.

The others went silent, wanting to know what Wingnut's question might be. He was always interested in stories of the past. The recruit seemed to have a thirst for such anecdotes.

'I'm told you blokes were once hit by a Tiger tank when you were in Italy. You survived the attack and all got out on that occasion, yet you lost mates in the first Matilda and the second Lee attacks. I'm presuming the Tiger tank attack, the third time you were unhorsed, was the most telling. I'm assuming the Tiger tank's shell was bigger than the Italian field gun's or that of the old Sturmgeschütz with its short barrel?'

'And you're wondering why so many of us in the Churchill tank got out?' replied McGrew.

'Well, yes,' Wingnut answered hesitantly. He knew the loss of past friends was something the tank crew felt deeply. He also sensed there was a strange bond among the four crewmen he had joined, four days ago.

'There would be a lot of variable reasons with that one, Wingnut.' McGrew offered the recruit a cigarette and then threw the pack to Meadows and gestured for him to pass the pack on to Louis and O'Hara.

The sergeant continued, 'The real reason is the Churchill tank has very thick armour and good escape hatches, especially at the side.' Then McGrew indulged himself with a laugh as he looked to Meadows. 'Once again, I recollect being pulled out of that side hatch by Meadows here. For the third time. My feet at ten to two, yet again, being dragged away from another burning tank. And there is me muttering…' McGrew stopped, waiting for his crew to respond.

Meadows, O'Hara and Louis all called back in unison, 'Déjà vu, déjà vu.'

The usual amused chortle of happy men followed.

'All five of us got out of that one. I remember our Louis here, shouting out some of his colourful expletives when he saw the distant Tiger tank rumble off over the craggy scarp, away to fight another day.'

'You still scolded me for bad language,' said Louis.

'I know, Louis. I just hate the F and C words. There is no place for such vulgar words,' added McGrew.

'Was Trooper Marks with you too? I presume he's one of the regular crew from North Africa and Italy?' Wingnut asked.

'Marks came to us just after Salerno. He'll see the shitshow out with his appendicitis occurring when it did. I think this shitshow will be finished in a few months. If not by us, then the Russians will do it.'

'That's when Meadows told us about our survivor's aurora,' said O'Hara.

'So he did,' added Louis. 'I remember that now. It was when you were dragging the sergeant away from the burning Churchill. I don't remember you saying the actual word *aurora*, but you did go a bit mystic about the whole thing, like a modern-day Merlin pretending that a spell for good was over us all.' He looked at Meadows who was frowning defensively.

'We're a tank crew,' said Meadows. 'Close and confined. Superstition comes with the territory. I think we might have someone watching over us, especially the sergeant and me. I'm his English valet, like Archibald Mulliner has in P.G. Wodehouse stories.' He grinned at Wingnut, hoping for approval. 'I'm the valet who pulls the sergeant out of burning tanks. It is pre-set by some all-knowing power.'

'There you go, Sergeant McGrew,' Louis laughed, 'your own valet to pull you out of tanks and stuff.'

'Well, it seems to have happened a few times.' Meadows laughed. 'It's almost a déjà vu circumstance, but not a joking matter when it's happening.'

'Certainly not the first time. That was the worst,' McGrew reminisced. For a moment the mood was destroyed – the silence became awkward and the sergeant realised he had soured the light-hearted part of the conversation. Perhaps he should resume and get it off his chest, all of the *almost* déjà vu experiences. 'Well now, you never know on those déjà vu matters. I remember I was very dazed on all three occasions. And my continued view of these unhorsing affairs is my bloody feet at ten to two and being pulled away from burning bloody tanks. I just don't want to hear that awful screaming again. The first one was by far the worst. I never want to witness that again.'

The entire atmosphere changed as more terrible and less humorous memories plagued the tank crew. The conversation had ended with the sombre memory of young Harry Edwards back in North Africa on that most dreadful of days, each wanting to move beyond the wicked moment to a kinder time.

McGrew began to gently sing…

Oh! I eat watermelon and I have for years,
sing Polly-wolly-doodle all the day;
I like watermelon but it wets my ears,
sing Polly-wolly-doodle all the day.

Maybe grass tastes good to a moo cow's mouth,
sing Polly-wolly-doodle all the day;

*But I like chicken 'cause I'm from the south,
sing Polly-wolly-doodle all the day.*

*Fare-thee well,
Fare-thee well,
Mister gloom be on your way.*

As the song continued, Meadows, O'Hara and Louis joined in. Wingnut watched them sing with melancholy voices, the tone of a sad and haunting experience. A dire memory filled with dread. The veteran crewmen indulged the kind memory of a departed young tank trooper – a young man they were all fond of. It made the new recruit nervous because he realised the song was for a nook containing a sorrowful memory. A moment for each trooper, lost. Wingnut also began to realise the tank crew suspected he might become a mere memory in the recess of each veteran's memory too. Perhaps one day, the recollection of his companionship would be contained within the song.

CHAPTER 5

A CANTER ACROSS THE STREAM

The cold afternoon air was refreshing as the tank formation rolled down the scarp and over the hard, frosty sod. Scattered snow patches were about here and there, evidence that the snowy winter was breaking. Perhaps the thaw would continue. Maybe there would be a fresh fall of snow.

Sergeant McGrew sat bolt upright as he peered out from the cupola hatch of Molly's turret. On either side of Molly's rumbling tracks was another Cromwell tank in shabby winter-white camouflage. One slightly ahead, the other a little behind. The green undercoat was grinning through on each Cromwell tank. Molly mare was the platoon's only tank not to have been given a coat of ghostly winter white. The tank following, called Mildred, was commanded by Corporal Chandler and travelled to the right. The other Cromwell tank, slightly forward, was called Jenny.

She was at the head of the arrowhead formation with first commander Lieutenant Samson. He was the platoon's new overall commander and travelled to the left. To the extreme left and back, almost level with Molly, was the supporting Firefly commanded by Staff Sharky. He rumbled along with the reconnaissance group, adding a little more firepower with a long seventeen-pounder gun barrel. The radio chatter had alerted them to the imminent appearance of Sergeant Davis' observation unit – they would soon break cover at the lower part of the scarp.

'We'll be like ships passing in the night,' muttered Louis as he drove Molly down the slope.

'Nags, Louis. Nags, me old mucker,' corrected Meadows light-heartedly.

Despite the sure knowledge of the observation tank breaking cover, McGrew was still amused to watch the distant Cromwell tank when it emerged from an admirably concealed position, seemingly out of nowhere from a huge holly bush.

McGrew pressed the B button on his microphone and spoke over the intercom. 'Well, that's a devilishly clever bit of cover for any observation tank to hide in. Did you clock that, Louis?'

'I did, Serge. Very crafty indeed,' crackled the reply of Molly's driver.

A smile creased McGrew's face as his rugged jaw twisted. He clicked the microphone back to the A setting and watched with professional admiration. The observation tank was covered in thick twigs and bracken. It looked like a giant hedgehog or one of Hobart's Funnies at such distance. McGrew assumed the tank must have been low down in a dip in the ground where the thick holly bushes grew over, looking like a relatively low-level and wide-spreading shrub – a thicket seemingly too low to hide a tank. But there had to be enough of a dip to cover a submerged vehicle that size, McGrew reasoned.

Close by, there was a small cluster of trees that overlooked the main river deep below and beyond. With the grey skies and the chilly bluster, there was a splendid outlook. McGrew supposed the spot would have been more idyllic in summer and during peacetime.

Molly was loudly rumbling along as part of the advancing tank troop – a clear approach view of the basin's lower meadows and another thin line of trees along the river bank. The little stream before them was gracefully trickling into the main river that arced away to the north east. The troop was still relatively safe on their side of the slope and the clusters of scattered thickets.

The observation tank was ascending towards them from the lower part of the gully with the little stream behind. It briefly took McGrew's mind away from the displeasing feeling of having his head above the cupola and fully exposed. He spared a thought for commander Davis and his crew of the observation unit. Their Cromwell made upwards to pass them by – their little mission was complete and they could return, back to the relative safety of their own line.

Lieutenant Samson's voice crackled over the radio. An instruction for Molly to hold the left flank.

McGrew pressed the B button on his microphone and spoke to Louis on the intercom, knowing his driver would have heard the chatter too. 'Drop back and move across to the left flank.' The sergeant immediately went back to the microphone's A setting as the tank formation rumbled on.

Louis called compliance from inside, above the rumbling noise, and smoothly dropped speed as the rest of the troop pushed on. He pulled the relevant steering lever back and Molly instantly veered behind the advancing arrowhead formation. She trundled to the extreme left and fell in beside the Firefly's left side, a manoeuvre handled with grace and experience.

Lieutenant Samson's head tank, Jenny, closed the gap left by Molly, dropping back. Sergeant McGrew remained sitting uncomfortably on his commander seat, his head still outside, looking over the turret and the gun barrel as the battalion of three Cromwell tanks and one Sherman Firefly rolled down the snow-scattered slope towards the dreaded frozen meadow with the wooded line on the other side of the shallow stream. All could hear the chatter of Lieutenant Samson reporting back to Squadron Headquarters over the broader radio net. The troop leader was making small reports as the scouting patrol edged along with the recon and pursuit mission.

Finally, the observation tank of Davis' troop rolled past them on its way up the slope in the opposite direction, Sergeant Davis giving McGrew a grim-faced wave as he went. The stern look conveyed a silent warning to remain guarded. McGrew even detected a slight shake of the head. It was enough of a warning for McGrew – something wasn't right. He and Davis went back a long way. His unit would need to be ready. McGrew wondered what he might do if there was an attack. Would the unbloodied troopers of the scouting patrol be up to it? Would the new platoon commander be calm in a storm? Of course, no one could fully prepare. Yet somehow, he knew this reconnaissance patrol wasn't going to pass without incident.

McGrew looked inside at Molly's crew and chose not to use the intercom. 'Sergeant Davis gave me a none too sure look, and a slight shake of the head,' he shouted down to Meadows over the rumbling noise. The others could hear, even above the tank's grumbling engine and the squealing of track wheels.

'He never reported anything,' replied Meadows nervously.

'That's because he never saw anything to report. It doesn't mean there's nothing there. Davis and Sharky think there is.' McGrew sighed.

'You got one of your bad feelings, Serge?' asked O'Hara.

'Keep your eyes peeled, Billy boy,' McGrew replied. 'You too, Louis, and you lads on the gun, keep an eye out too. Scan those bloody trees by the river. Drink in every inch.'

'Oh, aye – that's for sure,' replied O'Hara.

As the troop of tanks got closer to the stream, McGrew, Staff Sharky and Corporal Chandler, in charge of Mildred's crew, withdrew and lowered themselves inside their tanks for safety, closing their cupola hatches. McGrew noticed that Lieutenant Samson did no such thing.

'Another ruddy accident waiting to happen,' McGrew muttered to himself, continuing to watch the advance through the periscope. The crew tittered as they heard Lieutenant Samson instruct Staff Sharky to watch the woodland over the stream and along the left flank by the main river.

'It seems our young tank commander has a certificate in the apparent,' whispered Meadows sarcastically.

'Probably got it at university,' said O'Hara, chuckling.

'Enough there, lads. Keep your eyes peeled,' scolded McGrew quietly.

Each member of Molly's crew watched on various viewer scopes as ahead of them their lead commander's tank, Jenny, dropped down into the gully of the shallow stream.

'All stay focused on the woods,' Samson's instructions crackled over the intercom.

McGrew had to refrain himself from muttering something about sucking eggs. He also noted that Staff Sharky replied very politely over the radio net. The experienced man's West Country accent politely answered with a hint of sarcasm. No one was impressed by the new young officer Samson. Most of the non-commissioned officers felt the fledgling lieutenant was out of his depth. It wasn't the young man's fault. He was brave and determined, but he didn't have the experience of a survivor. Not yet. None of the troop were impressed by the previous officer either. Each of the troopers felt sad about the demise of such men, but officers didn't seem to last that long in their troop. Even the good ones.

Louis called through the din of the rolling track, warning them of the coming drop into the shallow stream gully. The driver let Molly's front down upon the shingle, the crew rolling with the expected front fall of the vehicle. The other tanks were already across the flowing shallows and climbing out of the gully. Molly followed, moving through the mere trickle of running water, crunching ice and shingle as her tracks continued to grind and roll forward. The iron nag pushed on, out on the rear left flank. Climbing the other side of the stream, the tank followed the advancing platoon rolling over the open meadow covered with scattered patches of snow, the pasture gently rising before them.

'Here comes the good bit,' muttered McGrew.

'Depends on what your idea of good is, Serge,' replied Meadows.

Wingnut was sitting, watching through his gunner's scope while Meadows, from his loader's position, checked the radio valves, knowing the jolting from the uneven ground could easily put the frequency setting out. He awaited further instructions from McGrew.

'Is the set holding out, Meadows?' McGrew asked light-heartedly.

Meadows smiled. 'She is, Serge – a right little tickety-boo darling of a radio set. If she was a bird, I'd pinch her little arse.'

Wingnut looked serious as he delivered his light-hearted punch line. 'If fair radio set were a fair lady, she would verily smote one 'twixt one's chops.'

There followed a moment of stunned silence to Wingnut's pretentious humour. It was just a second or two, but there was a slightly strained atmosphere until Louis broke the hush.

'He's a thespian,' called the driver humorously. 'An actor. He has been on the stage. I thought he had.'

'Yeah, on the stage, alright,' added Meadows. 'Probably sweeping it.'

'Keep your eyes on the woods there, lads,' added McGrew.

Amid the sniggers, each crew member did as instructed and continued to scrutinise the line of trees to their left as the platoon of tanks advanced up the gentle rise of the hill.

For his part, McGrew continued surveying the terrain ahead of the tank formation's advance. Instinct was kicking in and the veteran sergeant had a dreadful appreciation for the Sherman Firefly's more precarious position on this manoeuvre – Staff Sharky had a powerful seventeen-pound gun and the enemy knew this particular tank was the most formidable.

Lieutenant Samson called the order over the radio to fan out more and McGrew clicked to B to instruct Louis. It was already being done, but he still repeated the instruction to move a little more to the left, all the same. They were now closer to the cluster of trees where all suspected the main danger lurked, but each trooper knew that the enemy would likely target the Firefly and Samson's lead tank first. It would be at very close range and Molly's crew could only wonder at how nervous the forward crews must be.

'Load one! I want to be ready,' instructed McGrew through the intercom.

Wingnut swung in his seat ready as Meadows left the radio check and took a shell from the front profile container tray. He went through the breech action of loading the shell, yelling the drill the way he always did. Young Wingnut responded the way he had been taught. He seemed competent and well suited to the task, not fazed by the conditions yet. He received the light slap on the leg from Meadows – the shell was loaded and ready.

The platoon of tanks slowly moved up the gentle rise, each vehicle's tracks rolling over the damp pasture – making for the summit of the hill.

Again, McGrew spoke on the B intercom to his crew, 'Scan areas ten to eleven along the line of trees.'

Molly's turret turned slightly towards the approaching line of trees, as did the Firefly's and Jenny's, the lead tank.

Satisfied the movement was well executed, the entire crew were prepared, with Wingnut poised at the periscope and his right hand ready with the firing mechanism on standby, his eyes pressed up against the gunsight and the sweat running down his forehead. The whole confined space was suddenly very stuffy and the young gunner could feel more perspiration trickling down his back. The tension was intense and all were hoping for the release to come – one way or another. Molly continued to rumble slowly and cautiously along on the extreme left of the arrowhead formation.

'Any second now,' whispered McGrew to himself. He could sense what was coming. The entire crew could.

Then McGrew made out the flash of flame and a thin line of smoke spewing forward from inside the woods. There followed the explosive roar of a fireball erupting upon the front section of the Sherman Firefly. The rumbling tank came to an abrupt halt as thick black smoke and spitting flames quickly engulfed the hull of the stricken vehicle. The swirling dark cloud fanned out from the burning wreck.

'Eleven – four hundred!' roared McGrew, but he had forgotten to call on the B intercom setting. Everyone in Jenny and Mildred would hear the instruction. All except those inside the Firefly inferno, still screaming horrendously within the evil flames, their agonised death screams crackling over the radio's intercom.

'On it!' yelled Wingnut.

At the same instance, Molly's gun roared deafeningly and the shell hit directly where the enemy artillery shot was fired from. Wingnut was fast and had responded well – the lad hit something! A fireball erupted within the wood – an expanding balloon of wicked, engulfing orange flame mixed with black smoke.

Everything happened very quickly as Louis hissed, 'Oh, bloody hell!' The driver flinched fearfully before the abhorrent sight through his periscope, where Staff Sharky's Firefly had transformed into a raging firestorm. A human torch jumped from the burning tank and came staggering out through the black smoking plume, arms flailing about wildly as the wretched form agonisingly burned to death. A wicked but merciful burst of enemy machine-gun fire took the burning trooper down. Another burning figure emerged from the inferno and out of the black cloud, thrashing and screaming as a further concentrated clatter of machine-gun fire euthanised the soul of another pitiful trooper. There was no sign of the rest of the crew, just the desperate, high-pitched and tormented screams gradually fading over the crackling radio net. McGrew had switched on the A setting in case Lieutenant Samson called out instructions.

'Reload!' shouted McGrew, staring through his periscope for targets. He no longer cared about being on the A setting. His crew could hear him and when Lieutenant Samson wanted to respond, he could.

Meadows needed no instruction. He had already put the spent shell casing in a box. The efficient loader was already calling out his drill protocols. The second shell was in and the breech mechanism locked with his usual automatic efficiency – years of practice and now a mere reflex action under battle conditions. He slapped Wingnut's leg. The gun was ready. Go find a target!

O'Hara opened up on the Besa machine gun with swift precision, cutting a line of machine-gun fire around Wingnut's initial strike area, guiding the tracer to the fringe where he had seen enemy machine-gun fire. He grinned with vicious gratification as silhouettes in human form twisted and fell within his sure line of fire.

The wretched screams from the burning Firefly were gone. The radio intercom was now alive and crackling to a different sound – hoarse screams of unintelligible instructions from Lieutenant Samson. The officer was in panic mode and McGrew knew it. For the moment, it was useless trying to calm the irate young officer. Then there was a second artillery discharge to the right of Wingnut's strike and deeper into the wood.

'Eleven plus – five hundred!' yelled McGrew. Molly's crew understood their own unique jargon and Wingnut had been taught over the last four days. It was simple enough.

'Got it in sight!' shouted Wingnut, knowing Meadows' shouts that the loading drill was complete. The recruit fired upon the position with quick and impressive accuracy. Another erupting ball of expanding flame and smoke.

Again, O'Hara saturated the surrounding area with more machine-gun fire with an appalling inhuman grin revealing clenched side teeth and the front gap of missing incisors. His wicked blue eyes blazed with disgusting glee. 'Chew on this, yer bastards,' he hissed as more panic-stricken silhouetted foes were brought down by his cutting spray – the Grim Reaper's scythe cutting a diabolical harvest.

Within moments, the whole area was a battleground of flame and dreadful murder. Trading blast, strike and machine-gun fire for a reply of further blast, strike and machine-gun fire. Indiscriminate death and carnage, devouring all.

There were bullets pinging Molly's armour, but that was the least of the crew's worries. Meadows was calling out his third shell loading protocol. His confidence in his new gunner was growing.

'Good lad, Wingnut!' screamed McGrew. 'Louis, arc left and get us the hell out of here.'

Molly curved left in a rumbling sweep. Too quick and in panic could throw the tracks. Louis was mindful and controlled under fire. More projectiles smattered the tank's armour.

McGrew, Meadows and Wingnut rode the turning turret's swing as the gun rotated to cover Molly's retreat. The cannon was quickly repositioned and aiming over the rear right side, back at the woods. The lad was good – very good. Meadows was working well too. Amid the turning and mayhem of the battle, he had completed his third drill protocol and locked the breech with a slap on the gunner's leg. Another shell was in place and ready.

'Another beauty ready to kick arse,' said Meadows.

A third flash of enemy artillery fire resulted in an explosion of earth where Molly had just passed over while arcing left. Again, Wingnut's sight was upon the flash as he fired the third shot into the woods in the vicinity of the enemy discharge. He saw flame and earth erupt but no obvious strike. The shell had fallen a little short but the resulting explosion would hopefully cause enough confusion to buy the crew time to evade and get away.

'Troop – fall back! Troop – fall back!' Lieutenant Samson screamed over the radio net.

Mildred had fired a couple of shells and her machine gun was also blazing away into the woods.

McGrew winced and gritted his teeth as he watched through his periscope. The tracer spread took down more running silhouettes of two enemy combatants bathed in the brightness of Wingnut's burning carnage. He was impressed by the recruit's shooting. Perhaps there was an element of fortune while Molly was on the move, but the lad had done very well.

'Jenny's crew are unhorsed too. Completely down!' McGrew shouted. He witnessed the fleeting moment of horror through his own periscope. All about was fire and mayhem of raging battle – the enemy's destruction and casualties within the woods, and their own shocking casualties of the British tank platoon out on the open meadow.

McGrew watched on through the muck and fire of the vicious mêlée. He saw Lieutenant Samson manage to climb out of the cupola. The officer lingered on the turret of the burning tank and bravely turned to try and pull another crewman out. Samson's lead Cromwell was ablaze with flames licking about the stricken tank's left side. Jenny was finished. It was just a matter of seconds before…

Samson spasmodically jerked and arched his back. Enemy bullets had struck him. Further machine-gun projectiles hit the young officer as he spun around, a spiralling spray of speckled red mist fanning out from his stricken and twisting form. Lieutenant Samson fell from the turret onto the hard sod. The young troop commander lay dead as a second shell hit the already stricken Jenny. The radio net didn't pick up the horrendous screams on this occasion. Perhaps the remaining crew inside the burning vehicle were dead. Or perhaps the radio system was already smashed.

'Get us out of here, Louis,' yelled McGrew. 'This bit of the shitshow is over.'

More bullets pinged off Molly's armour while the crew roughly bounced about inside the tank. The smell of cordite from the fired shells was becoming overwhelming and nauseating when mixed with the enhanced smell of fuel. The dreaded combustible air of Molly's inner compartment, air that would ignite with a shell strike. Each trooper's face was etched with concern. An anxious gnawing of resolve – a battle against outright panic. The earth erupted a few feet to the tank's right side. The unknown enemy gunner wasn't as good as Wingnut – thankfully.

A fourth shell was loaded, Meadows screaming the protocols through all the mayhem. Wingnut remaining focused and received another leg slap for completion. The recruit had already found his target, but the bouncing and movement of Molly in haste made it hard to keep the retreating target in focus. He let loose with the shell anyway. If the shot missed, it would at least keep some heads down and buy more precious seconds to put distance between themselves and the area of conflict. He heard the explosion but the turret was already turning to put the long gun barrel facing forward with the direction of escape. Now, in cavalry jargon, Molly's wheels and tracks were galloping off in hasty retreat.

The remaining Cromwell tanks, Molly and Mildred, rumbled back towards the stream. Amid the fighting retreat, each tank accelerated to full speed. The increased momentum over the rough terrain caused continued discomfort as all anxiously sprang about. Crew members clutched what they could to steady themselves as each of the iron mounts trundled over the uneven ground.

Louis opened the small circular driving hatch before him. The inrush of cold winter air swishing into his face was extremely gratifying, cold fresh air that blustered past into the confines of the tank. A cold rush to battle the sickening smell of cordite and fuel.

McGrew managed to lift the cupola hatch while clinging to his raised chair frame with one hand. The smell of fumes and acrid cordite was swept away – a crude but effective ventilator system had come into effect. Meadows opened his loader's hatch too as the sergeant reached over the radio set and grabbed the flare gun. He aimed out of the cupola and fired a blazing trail of expanding smoke into the air. McGrew tried to cling to his raised chair while desperately trying to reload as the tank roughly dipped and bobbed over the rough terrain. The desperate sergeant smashed against the breech and then fell back against the radio rack within the confined turret area. Yet, somehow, he managed to accomplish his task of reloading the flare gun. Another shot fired out of the open hatch to spread smoke out into the winter air.

The thick grey haze fanned out to obscure their rushed retreat from the enemy forces in the woodland. Hopefully, their adversaries could no longer make out where Molly was.

The enemy guns continued to fire at Mildred as she rumbled along at speed. Not one of her crew had managed to fire any smoke flares. O'Hara could see that the spread of their own cover would take some time to obscure Mildred's desperate run.

'Mildred is still exposed,' he shouted.

McGrew called out, 'Did you hear Chandler on the net? He managed to radio Squadron HQ.'

'I think he was asking for an artillery barrage,' called Meadows.

'We're approaching the stream's embankment at a speed there, Louis,' Wingnut said nervously.

'Louis!' McGrew shouted over the pandemonium. Everyone was being thrown about. Molly's bouncing suspension was working flat out as she sped over the bumpy ground. The sergeant gave up shouting and managed to load a third flare as he was flung about. He aimed through the open cupola and fired again into the grey sky. Hopefully, the thick emission was aiding their desperate and full-blooded retreat.

'I think Chandler has just managed to fire a flare too,' Louis called out as the rumbling tank jostled and bolted along.

'Too blooming right,' yelled Meadows. 'We're running like blue-arsed flies.'

'That one works for me, that's for sure!' screamed O'Hara.

'Even I could have told the top brass that was going to happen. We all knew it would,' roared Louis as Molly seemed to pick up more speed, coupled with more unbearable bouncing over the rough land. He was moderately zigzagging as best he could towards a rapidly approaching line of saplings on the stream's bank.

O'Hara turned and looked nervously at Louis as another shell exploded close to their right. Earth, smoke and fire retreated via the rear viewer.

'That one was blooming close,' muttered O'Hara, clearly nervous as he decided the line of trees was nearing much faster than he would have liked.

Louis had straightened up and was pushing Molly at a breakneck pace for the final stretch – the area where a small precipice dropped into the stream's gully – at a speed of almost forty miles an hour that none of the violently bobbing crew had ever experienced.

O'Hara looked behind nervously and saw Wingnut tightly embracing the breech with all its jiggered edges while Meadows was clutching the profile armament trays with their remaining shells inside. McGrew was clinging to a section of the radio bracket's casing while still bouncing up and down. Each crewman wore the same look of petrified dread.

Someone shouted out, 'Sod this for a blinking lark!'

O'Hara watched as the other Cromwell, Mildred, began to roar ahead of them. Yet another enemy shell exploded and struck the earth right between the faster vehicle's rear sprockets. O'Hara and Louis watched the terrible event with abject dismay. Time seemed to slow down for the split second when each trooper watched the steel monster come to an abrupt halt. The whole burning back section of the tank was raised sharply with the force of the sudden stop and the lift of the rear explosion. The burning Cromwell seemed to stop upright upon her front, the long gun barrel moving the turret sideways as the end of the gun pressed into the ground. O'Hara and Louis expected the entire tank to turn over completely. The iron brute was like a bucking horse. All of the back stowage – rolled coverings and various tools fixed outside – was cast off and over the vehicle. For a moment, the tank's rear stood upright at almost ninety degrees. It lingered as though the metal nag was making its mind up which way to fall. Then the stricken Cromwell fell back onto her tracks as Molly sped past the flaming monument – the last tank of the platoon bouncing along at the limit of her Merlin engine's power.

O'Hara gasped as he watched through his turning periscope. 'Shit! Chandler's unhorsed,' he yelled and then they heard the clatter of more machine-gun fire, probably cutting down any troopers trying to bail out. They heard another explosion but couldn't see the further demise of Mildred.

Louis tried to press his foot further down on the accelerator, but it was already at its speed limit. The ground became bumpier as the crew crashed about more violently than ever. All were shouting at Louis in panic. The whole affair was becoming increasingly desperate. Another shell exploded to the left of them, and O'Hara's voice called out in panic.

'Slow down, Louis!'

'No bloody chance! Hold on to your arses, lads, we're going for the full gallop and jump! Right over the gully and into the next field!'

There followed a cacophony of panicking protestations from the desperate crew, clutching at anything with sharp-cornered metal fixings because that was all their dire circumstances offered.

Sergeant McGrew started to desperately call out an instruction when Molly sped off the rising lip of the gully's precipice. His voice was lost in a bubble of awe. The tank had launched herself serenely into the void. For that little moment of astonished gulps, it all went quiet. The surreal sensation of twenty-eight tons of metal nag majestically cruising through the air and over the stream. A moment of peculiar calm. An instant frozen in time and stretched out to savour for a few split seconds. Split seconds that seemed to go by very slowly indeed. A time to think of the unappetising prospect of impact upon landing. The stark realisation of Sergeant McGrew's voice screaming at Louis over the intercom, 'Declutch! Declutch!'

CHAPTER 6

MOLLY THE MOST RESPLENDENT MOUNT

Molly had rumbled to a halt upon the frozen earth after her twenty-eight tons of metal hit the ground and literally bounced upon her severely tested suspension. Her hurried forty-mile-an-hour momentum propelled her wheeled mass forward on her neutral declutched base. All this happened as the Allied lines opened up with a terrific bombardment upon the enemy position. Now the Cromwell tank was motionless, waiting to respond to her crew's next wish. For the moment, it was awfully quiet inside – very quiet, indeed.

Molly the tank remained still upon the frozen earth as the Allied guns started to bomb in unison, explosions erupting in lines all along the small stretch of the enemy-held treeline. The protecting shells whistled over the divide and beyond the Cromwell tank's position to drop upon the enemy's woodland location. The ferocious bombardment of the woods ensued. The very woods that Molly's tank crew had fled from. Eruptions of earth, fire and smoke now covered the crew's desperate escape. Outside of the fire-erupting woodlands sprawled the smouldering ruins of the three wrecked Allied tanks. The Firefly and two Cromwells. The twisted and scattered forms of dead crew lay grotesquely about the burning debris of each vehicle. Wasted troopers cut down in the prime of their lives. More enemy troops within the exploding woodland being taken in their prime. An obscure episode of combat in a massive war. A low-key event that would be unheard of in the broader and more dreadful picture of a war. Something minor and not worthy of note. But then Molly's crew didn't think in such a way.

Inside the tank came groans of pain and discomfort amid the confining darkness. Outside it sounded like the end of the world. Their own side's shells were raining down, each explosion within and about the fringe of the enemy-held woodland.

'Molly hit the ruddy frozen earth like a grossly overweight lady. A fat old tart with delusions of being a gymnast,' groaned Meadows, painfully holding his ribs. His nose was bleeding but he couldn't feel anything broken. He managed to stand and re-open his loader's hatch that had slammed shut upon landing. Light and the enhanced sound of the bombardment flooded inside.

'A fat bitch summersaulting and dropping from parallel bars. Rather badly, in my opinion,' groaned Wingnut. He felt his bloodied nose and was pleased it wasn't broken, though it had taken a severe bang. His left wrist was also bruised and his right thigh was tingling and numb from another impact. Somehow, he had clung to the gun breech with all its blocks and lumps ready and waiting for the bouncing trooper's soft, yielding flesh. The thickness of his pixie suit and under garments had helped, coupled with his tight embrace. How he wasn't further injured was beyond him. But he was glad to come out of the ordeal as he had done.

'Sergeant McGrew is not saying anything,' muttered O'Hara from the darkness of his compartment. There was a note of concern. 'He went flat down and grabbed something, but I think he bounced upwards when we first hit the ground and then got slung about with the tank's uneven roll.'

'We bounced first and then hit the ground rolling,' replied Louis.

Meadows managed to sit the tank commander up. McGrew instantly began to come around. There was a nasty bump on his head, just above his left eye, almost like he had been hit in the head by a stone.

He reached up to touch the lump and groaned as he felt more pain in his ribs and stomach.

'What the blooming hell is that noise?' asked McGrew between hisses of pain as he reached around to feel the small of his back.

'It's our lot, Serge,' replied Louis. 'They're raining down heavy on the woodland. Nice big "bugger off" shells, all for Jerry.'

'They're very welcome to them,' groaned O'Hara.

'They could have done that before sending us out to scout around,' McGrew cursed.

'They're always wise after the event,' agreed O'Hara.

'We landed like a fat tart sitting down fast on bricks,' McGrew continued.

'I feel like that fat bird's arse then,' complained Wingnut.

'Let's get some more light in here. The cupola hatch must have slammed shut,' said McGrew over the continuous bombardment going on outside. The shells were screaming over and above their position, continuing to pound the enemy-held woodland.

O'Hara pushed open his side door and roof section to allow for more light. All were greeted by the comical sight of his broken nose and two black eyes. What made the image more amusing was that O'Hara seemed oblivious to his injuries.

'You know, Billy O'Hara,' McGrew said, laughing in some discomfort, 'you always had that look of a bloke who's been put through a meat grinder and come out the other side. But now, you look like you have decided to run back and have a second go, like a little kid playing on a park slide.'

O'Hara treated them all to his big ugly toothless grin and it served them well. The ludicrous sight of the battered face seemingly uncaring of such looks set off titters of amusement.

'I can't get over this one,' began Wingnut. 'Dropping out of the sky in such an apparatus. Landing on the frozen earth belly first. The majesty of the tonnage calmly sailing through the air then suddenly it was rudely snatched away. That was one blooming eerie sensation.' He started to giggle and cough.

'I'm not sure if she's broken,' said Louis. 'She has unceremoniously bounced. That would extensively strain any suspension carrying this weight. Yet somehow, Molly seems to have held.'

'Seems to have held?' Meadows asked in a sarcastic but enquiring manner. 'I can't believe the radio valves are still working.' He aligned the frequency setting.

'Well,' added Louis, looking thoughtful. 'Molly rumbled along on her protesting tracks for a short way after bouncing, and then came to a halt. I did declutch as we went into the air.'

'Well, if that don't take the blooming biscuit,' moaned Meadows sarcastically. 'Give the driver a bleeding medal!'

Louis scolded back, 'You're a bit battered and bruised, but that's a hell of a lot better than being back there with the rest of the troop.'

O'Hara had seen the demise of the other tanks and lent his voice in support. 'Louis got us out of that one, that's for sure, Meadows.'

Outside, the bombardment continued but within the confines of Molly's iron armour, Meadows wanted to continue his moaning.

'Might I say, as a devoted member of this crew, it never felt like an experience in that same eloquent way you put it, Louis. Molly bouncing and rumbling along to a fairy-tale stop? Not inside this iron box with all its metal bits and pieces here, there and everywhere. Except where you're sitting, perhaps. You had the best seat in the place. So "arseholes" to your jolly romp account of a nice little declutched bouncing tank.'

McGrew decided to resume his command with a strong rebuke. 'Wind yer neck in and get on with yer blooming knitting, Meadows. We are all here and we need to move on.'

Everyone was injured, bruised and winded. Each crew member was in pain from some bump or other. But amazingly, only O'Hara had a broken nose. It had been broken before and it meant nothing to the tough little auxiliary machine gunner.

McGrew quickly gathered his wits and put aside the discomfort of his various injuries. 'We can't rely on the ceaseless discord outside. It will stop soon.' He raised himself and felt the displeasure of his bruises inflame. Gritting his teeth, he moved forward to look through his periscope. He could see the gentle rise of the scarp dotted with scattered trees and thickets.

'Hey, Louis. Can you see that thick wide-spreading holly bush at the beginning of the rise? Close to the cluster of trees?'

'That was where Davis had his observer position,' Louis replied.

'The very one. See if Molly will start up and make for the cover there.'

'We can use Davis' little observation hideout,' said O'Hara with another comical grin.

Louis fired up the tank and gently moved Molly forward at a slow pace while listening intently to the rumble of the tracks. The forward motion was slow and cautious but then there came a worrying sound of track slap. The hits lasted for a few turns before the driver halted. The tank's Merlin engine was still rolling over in neutral as Louis turned to McGrew.

'Something's wrong with one of the tracks. At least one of the links, anyway. Did you hear the track slap? I don't know how bad or how far we can get. And it's on my driver's side.'

'Right, everyone else dismount and take a look along the tracks on Louis' side. O'Hara, check your side, just in case,' barked McGrew sternly. He accepted that Louis knew every sound of Molly's workings and if he said a track link wasn't right, he would be correct in such an assumption.

O'Hara climbed out of his side opening, and Meadows climbed out of his loader's hatch with Wingnut following. The cold air was consoling, even though the overhead bombardment and continued explosions forced each trooper to crouch nervously. Wingnut was already checking along the track to the rear and stopped by the sprocket wheel. He looked up at McGrew who was staring back at him from the cupola hatch.

'I think the dodgy link is here,' called Wingnut. 'You might be able to limp Molly to the big bush by the trees, where you said Sergeant Davis' observation unit was located. But, once there, we'll need to change the link and replace other links either side of the damaged one. Three links in all, Serge.'

McGrew ducked his head inside the tank and called to Louis. 'Wingnut reckons we can limp it forward to the observation unit's thicket cover before we change three track links. That would be a safer bet. How do you feel about it?'

Louis nodded and replied loudly above the falling barrage and explosions across the stream, where Molly had made her grand leap. 'We'll need to take it slowly then and hope the bombardment keeps going as we edge along. Right now, that shower of shells is all we have to cover our retreat. We'll have to hope no Jerry observer is brave enough to look over their covering positions.'

'I'll tell them to keep an eye on the link as we move slowly forward then, that's for sure.' McGrew raised his head once more outside of the cupola and gave the instructions to be vigilant as the tank slowly moved forward. In the same instance, Louis engaged the gears and Molly rolled forward at a crawling pace.

Meadows grinned at Wingnut. 'A right bag of laughs this one's turning out to be. Another little anecdote for later.'

Wingnut took no notice of the amusing statement. His concern was with the loose and crushed link he could see moving along the top just beneath the vendor. The Cromwell had no upper supporting wheels to cushion the roll of the track.

'That's a big area of free swing between the back sprocket and that little raised front wheel. Gently does it now, Molly,' muttered Wingnut nervously.

'Yeah, it is,' agreed Meadows as he watched the vibration of the upper track moving along. 'The centre section is where it'll be slacker.'

'Well, it's just past that bit and now it's going around the little front wheel. Slowly does it. There's a good girl, Molly.' Wingnut gritted his teeth as the imperfection of the damaged link passed around the little wheel and slowly descended under the first of the big wheels.

'Now it's got the full twenty-eight tons pressing down on it,' said Meadows.

'That might be helpful,' replied Wingnut. 'I think the next test will be when the damaged track is hooked on the sprocket again.'

Meadows looked ahead at the ground rising before the tank and the cluster of trees where the wide-spreading thicket was. 'Blimey, we still have an awful long way to go. And our Molly's going at a snail's pace. I hope our boys keep dropping that payload on Jerry. Just to keep his head down.'

'Keep your arse cheeks clenched and hope for the bombardment to last,' said O'Hara, laughing. He had been picking up some of the stowage that had come apart from the tethers when Molly had landed and bounced upon her tested suspension. Many of the stowage items were lying about in the wake of the tank's roll. The small rough-looking trooper walked to the rear of the tank carrying the most precious of discarded items – the crew's valuable Jerry box stamped with its small emblem depicting an open-winged eagle perched upon an encircled swastika. He slung the container onto the back of Molly and then joined Meadows and Wingnut to watch the slow progress.

'I reckon there are a few arses that have taken a bashing during this little scout,' Meadows said.

'Well, let's hope ours are up to this one. We're lucky the ground is hard and frozen without much earth clinging to the tracks. Less weight is a help along the top run,' added Wingnut as he winced at the sight of the damaged track link moving onto the sprocket. It held, once again, slowly moving across the vast area of vibrating slack between the rear sprocket and the raised front wheel. Each turn of the track becoming a moment of dread before the damaged area rolled beneath the big wheels for what, the crew believed, was a moment of respite. Then the entire test, all over again, along the top vibrating run. They followed the slow progress inch by inch, while above the shells continued to pass and drop on the enemy.

'I'll leave you lads to watch it,' said O'Hara. He had quickly tired of watching the track link and went back to collecting some more displaced stowage scattered across the grass. Anything else retrievable was just an added bonus against the battered and recovered Jerry box – the big container with its precious cargo of tea, sugar and various edibles.

Gradually, they began to take heart as Molly lumbered up the scarp, moving ever closer to her goal –

the tantalising widely spread thicket by the fringe of the young silver birch trees – a rise that overlooked the main river. Each of the troopers watched on while Sergeant McGrew stared down at their anxious faces waiting for one of them to call up, in alarm. Thankfully, the expected appeal never came and they reached the thicket and slowly rolled beyond to a stop. They needed to ponder their next move and reverse inside the opening of the bush pointing away from the bombardment and the enemy's view.

'Why is the entrance facing our own lines?' Wingnut asked.

McGrew climbed out and jumped down. 'It's better our fellas can see it than the enemy, Wingnut.' He walked to the front of the tank, where Louis had popped his head outside of the open driver's trap doors.

'Will we be able to do the tracks beneath that giant shrub? It looks like a good overhang inside the entrance with a big area under the natural canopy.' Louis was suddenly more enthusiastic.

McGrew held a finger up and replied, 'I'll get O'Hara to take a look.' He then turned to the auxiliary machine gunner. 'Billy, see if the area of concealment in the bush will allow room for the necessary track changes.'

O'Hara jogged behind the tank and into the opening. He dropped out of sight and seemed to have gone underground. Within seconds he was back up and calling.

'It's ideal, Serge. And below ground. There's a big bowl-shaped dip down here. Molly can hide to her heart's content.'

'Bloody smashing!' said Meadows with McGrew nodding and smiling agreeably.

'Hold on a moment there, Louis,' called O'Hara as he went to the back of the tank and retrieved the valued Jerry box. 'We'll not want this falling off when you reverse.'

Meadows grinned and put a thumbs up. 'Too right, Billy boy.'

Louis needed no further instruction as he put Molly into reverse and slowly edged her backwards towards the hole under the wide-spreading thicket. O'Hara signalled from one side of the reversing tank while McGrew walked along the other side, waving the delicate manoeuvre along. Meadows and Wingnut followed Molly's reversing front end and whistled with delight as her metal bulk suddenly dropped down an incline inside the entrance.

Wingnut whistled impressively. 'Bloody hell! You would never know Molly was there. That dip is a blinder of an advantage when it comes to camouflage and concealment.'

Overhead, the shells continued their offensive flight, exploding beyond the stream that ran into the main river, amid the enemy's wooded position. It was pure hell on earth. No one of the tank crew envied the poor souls trying to evade such an onslaught, even if the wretched people were the enemy.

McGrew called to Meadows and Wingnut and pointed around. 'I want that big tree trunk over there and all that loose bush looking like tumbleweed. It's what Davis had over the front of his tank when he pulled out. It will be added cover by this entrance. It all helps.' He was grinning enthusiastically.

Meadows and Wingnut jumped to the task and in quick time the tree trunk and the bushes were lying along Molly's front with netting from their stores weighing down the bracken and natural debris spread across it.

Louis climbed out of his hatch and all stood in the opening with thick holly arching over and above them. It was at that moment the bombardment ceased and the radio crackled into life. McGrew withdrew into the tank while Meadows clambered up and dropped in through the loader's hatch.

'Did they stop when we got inside this cover?' asked Wingnut concerning the bombardment.

'I reckon so,' replied O'Hara.

'It would be a big coincidence if they didn't see us enter,' said Louis.

'So that entire bombardment was for our benefit?' Wingnut seemed surprised.

'I think the enemy-held woodland was the prime target, but I imagine our observers saw us trying to make for this spot and decided to lend a little help by continuing the bombardment longer than necessary,' Louis replied as he removed his spectacles and began to clean them.

'Aye,' agreed O'Hara. 'It made Jerry keep his head down and filled the area with fire and smoke. It all helped to conceal us.'

Louis put his glasses back on. He then walked along the side of the tank to the back of the bushy cavern. Wingnut and O'Hara followed him. They looked out through the twigs to across the basin. The stream that Molly leaped seemed at quite a distance. But it was the sight of the enemy-held woodland that made them gasp. As the smoke cleared, they saw the woodland was all but gone. An area of smashed trees lying about like a mass of broken matchsticks.

'Bloody hell,' said Wingnut, surveying the shorn-off tree trunks and the pockmarked earth. The smoke had begun to thin and the utter devastation was apparent to all.

'I can see Staff Sharky's Firefly, Chandler's and Lieutenant Samson's tanks too. All unhorsed yet somehow we cleared the jump and got to the finishing line,' said O'Hara.

'More mates gone. Wilson was with Lieutenant Samson's crew. He was a North Africa and Italy man,' replied Louis.

Wingnut began to realise that his two friends were riding the loss of close friends, something that had become a wicked second nature to them. He supposed they would be the same way about him and accepted that they expected it to happen. They had seen it all too often.

CHAPTER 7

SOME MORE UNWELCOME NEWS

Molly's track repair had moved along nicely. The three men of the tank crew were rather pleased and invigorated by the swift progress. The damaged link was almost in exactly the right place for the required work to be done. Molly had needed just a few feet more of reverse. There was enough room within the thicket cover for the manoeuvre. O'Hara mentioned that he wished he had such luck, the next time he was in Civvy street, when visiting a horse-racing venue. All three had just finished the lever work with the track adjust idler, and work on the last remaining track pin was the final part of the maintenance work.

'I can't believe this one,' Meadows groaned as he jumped down beside the work party. They were engrossed with the final stage, their interest on O'Hara hammering in the final pin link.

'What is it now?' asked Louis nonchalantly.

'Serge has just been on the radio to report to Troop Command. They've told us to stay put and continue to observe the enemy position.'

'What, the position they've blown to kingdom come?' asked Wingnut.

Meadows nodded. 'They want us to keep lookout and report if there is any sign of movement. We are to remain concealed and in here.'

'Why would there be any movement after that bombardment?' Wingnut was perplexed.

'Jerry will send another group into the unclaimed area before we take it,' Louis answered his innocent question.

'That means we're *not* moving forward today,' O'Hara muttered. He turned back to hammering the final part of the track pin. The loud clink sounding louder within the overhang of the huge holly bush. He looked back after the third and last thump of the sledgehammer. 'Almost like a workshop in here,' he muttered satisfactorily.

Meadows chuckled anxiously. 'Now, you're bang on the money with your "stay put today" notion. We're going to be here all bloody night, on observation and listening within the divide of this bloody stand-off.'

McGrew climbed out of the cupola and jumped down beside the group. He was clasping a pair of binoculars.

'Is it going to be an all-night job, Serge?' O'Hara asked.

'It seems that way, Billy. It will mean we're not going to be with the advance. I think that is going to happen tomorrow morning.'

'Did you ask?' Again, Wingnut's inexperience showed.

'Don't be so naïve, young Wingnut,' replied McGrew. 'HQ is not going to be telling me things like that, now. And I'm not going to be asking such things from HQ over the radio. They're not in the habit of informing lone sergeants and their tank crews about top-brass things. I'm just guessing, lad, that's all.'

He pulled a pack of cigarettes from the pocket of his dirty pixie suit and offered them around after putting one in his mouth. They all ambled to the back of the tank and sat down on the cold earth's dip, all secure in the knowledge that they were covered by the holly canopy and the natural trench. Each man took turns to receive a light for his cigarette.

'We will be here for the night at least. We are to observe and keep a look out for Jerry doing any night-time movement. As we know from past experience, Jerry will try to reposition during the darkness and will, no doubt, be expecting an advance from us. I also want to be exceptionally vigilant during this watch because I think it's very feasible that Jerry might try to sneak up here. The wood to the sides clearly overlooks the river and approach road, all the way to the bend where the pontoon bridge is. I can't understand why they didn't use the position before.'

Meadows made a valid comment. 'Perhaps the burnt-out Jerry Sturmgeschütz we saw back at the line was here? Maybe Jerry pushed his luck and went further uphill, where he could get a better view of the pontoon bridge?'

'But instead, got a taste of Polish vengeance,' added Wingnut.

'Aye,' agreed O'Hara. 'That makes sense. A few shots at the pontoon bridge and not expecting the advance Polish battalion to be lurking in the woods above.'

'It all starts to form a little picture of events,' Louis agreed.

'It does, that's for sure.' Sergeant McGrew drew on his cigarette and blew out a thin satisfying stream of smoke.

'Do you all think Jerry will come back this far? Right up here to the cluster of trees beside this bush we're sitting in?' Wingnut was enjoying being enlightened by the experienced men of his unit. He listened with great interest.

'Of course,' answered Louis. 'We've seen Jerry do such things before. Especially in Italy.'

McGrew supported the answer and spoke directly. 'Jerry is good, Wingnut. As you must realise by now, the devious sods are no mugs and they will do anything to hamper our advance. A recce up the slope during the night is very feasible and we must remain very vigilant.'

Meadows added to the debate. 'We are to inform HQ of any potential movement – anything at all.'

'It will also get bloody cold as I'm sure you are aware. We can't leave the engine running out here. We'll have blankets and coats on but Molly's lighting won't be used. We still have those little enclosed candle lanterns.'

'Candle lanterns?' Wingnut asked.

'We salvaged a couple back in France,' said Meadows. 'Better them than using Molly's lighting. No unnecessary use of Molly's battery power when stationary and switched off.'

McGrew smiled and winked at Meadows and Wingnut. 'Well, that's about the size of it then, lads. I want Wingnut and Meadows out here for the first watch. O'Hara and Louis can get a nice brew going. If we are to remain here, we may as well get comfortable.'

O'Hara and Louis needed no second instruction. They would throw the old tea slops over the soil and start a new brew. Each trooper climbed upon Molly then dropped inside to start the accepted tea-making chore. A chore they seemed happy to comply with.

'Well, it'll not take them long to be back here with a brew,' said McGrew as he stamped his cigarette out and stood up, rubbing his legs against the February chill. He also gingerly touched the large bruised bump above his eye, checking the throbbing ache and deciding to get some ointment from the medical box if it got worse. He peered through the holly foliage and out over the basin towards the bombarded woods across the stream. There were still scattered fires. Staff Sergeant Sharky's wrecked Firefly remained smoking. The two Cromwell tank wrecks were just burnt-out blackened hulks with their fellow troopers scattered about, lying dead.

McGrew sighed as he raised the binoculars to observe better. He allowed his vision to scan the shorn trees and the devastation of the area. He noted four enemy soldiers crawling among the strewn tree stumps.

The sergeant whistled with surprised respect. 'Well now! There go some crafty bastards. Our devoted enemy is already crawling back into position. That didn't take long. They look like scruffy old sods. Their coats look massive. Huge great baggy things, one brown and two grey, and one in a black civilian trench coat. They look almost civilian in attire but they are all holding weapons. Wearing different-coloured ski caps too. A black and grey one, but the black civilian trench-coat job is wearing a grey steel helmet. These are an odd ball lot. They must be from a right old mishmash bunch, that's for sure.'

'Jerry does love a ski cap,' admitted Wingnut.

'Perhaps blokes from different regiments pieced together? Jerry does like to improvise too. That's something we've learned over the years.' Meadows stood up next to McGrew and was handed the binoculars.

'Down there.' The sergeant pointed through the foliage and added, 'Just at about one o'clock from the wreck of Mildred.'

Meadows caught the swift movement of enemy soldiers quickly crawling under and over horizontal smashed trunks of silver birch trees. 'Our Jerry's not one to back off lightly. The bastards are getting ready for the next round. However, I make you right. They don't look experienced or that fit. They don't move like trained regulars.'

'Can I have a look?' asked Wingnut.

Meadows handed the recruit the binoculars and pointed through the foliage. 'Follow the line from the blackened remains of Mildred at—'

'One o'clock,' Wingnut finished. He put the optics to his eyes and immediately saw a lot of movement amid the debris of broken trees and sporadic fires. 'Bloody hell. There're quite a few of the bastards. They're like bleeding rats. Old blokes and some very young lads. The boys look about twelve or thirteen in oversized clothing. Some of the old ones are wearing civilian hats and flat caps! They've all got armbands.'

'They make for sorry-looking rats,' replied Meadows with remorseful indignation.

'The light is fading and I reckon it might be a good idea to let HQ know. They might drop another pile of shit on the bastards,' McGrew said. 'Keep watch on them. I'm going back inside to make the call.'

Moments later, Louis was before them with two piping hot mugs of tea. 'Serge reckons Jerry is crawling about the woodlands.'

'What's left of the woods,' corrected Wingnut with a smile. He took his mug of tea and handed Louis the binoculars. 'Follow anywhere from twelve o'clock to three o'clock from Mildred's wreck.'

This time, Louis whistled. 'I can't believe our lot haven't caught that. They don't look much good to me.'

'I reckon our lot are watching it with great interest,' replied Meadows. 'They might as well let Jerry put more of their ragtag soldiers in place before we drop another load on them.'

Wingnut spoke up. 'Jerry must realise we can do it again. Why are they using infantry to hold back an expected tank attack? There are no more artillery batteries or tanks supporting them now. They do realise they're up against tanks, don't they?'

Wingnut appreciated being able to ask questions of his experienced troopers. In response, the veterans seemed to delight in answering him. Even if they thought his enquiries were sometimes juvenile, they would always indulge him.

Louis threw further light on the matter as he easily spotted the obvious and inexperienced movement of the soldiers. 'I think the troops are those new types we've been informed about from briefings. The Americans have reported such soldiers to the south. I think they might be *Volkssturm* – a national militia. That is desperate. As for your question about knowing they face tanks. I think they are very aware. Those long pole-shaped things with the fat ends some of them are carrying – they are *Panzerfaust* anti-tank. They're a quick and disposable form of weapon. Easy to learn and easy to use.'

'So, they have an ability of sorts, then?' Wingnut seemed in fearful awe.

Meadows shook his head disapprovingly. 'Oh Christ, even untrained blokes can use those things. They can be very effective at close range. If this bottom-of-the-barrel brigade of nutters are naïve to soldiering, and I think the youngsters will be, their delusionary braveness might give them that little bit extra on the arsehole front. That could serve them well at the start of the fight.'

'Until they get their rude awakening,' added Louis. 'I imagine our blokes will have to knock it out of them rather swiftly. This is not going to be pretty.' Louis looked to the recruit, Wingnut. Then he added, 'We've got front-seat tickets to what's going to be a very messy and bloody, ugly performance.'

'So, we must be in Germany then? They wouldn't have these militia if we were still in Holland.' Wingnut's nervous interest could not be contained.

Meadows replied sarcastically, 'That certificate in the apparent is coming in handy, Wingnut. Did you get it from the late Lieutenant Samson?'

'Let's not speak ill of the dead,' added Wingnut solemnly.

'Even if it is in jest, it's rather bad taste, Meadows,' Louis agreed.

Meadows sighed. 'Alright, lads – point taken. For the record, Wingnut, *Volkssturm* are like our Home Guard. At least I think they are. That is a turn up for the books. Let's be honest, Jerry must be in a bit of shit, around these parts, if they're using Home Guard types so soon.'

'I think we should tell Sergeant McGrew while he's informing HQ on the radio,' said Louis. He returned the binoculars to Meadows then went back to Molly and clambered up onto the turret, an unusual entry point for the driver.

'Don't get giddy, Louis,' called Meadows humorously.

'I'll try not to.' He smiled and got down on his knees to call into the cupola. 'Serge, we think the soldiers are *Volkssturm*. Like those lot we were informed about a few days ago. The lot the Yanks sent the memo about. Their people have seen them down south. They look like old blokes dressed in bits of shabby uniform, like some Home Guard outfit. They look inexperienced, but are very well tooled up with weaponry, especially those *Panzerfaust* anti-tank weapons.'

Suddenly, O'Hara's ugly head appeared. He was holding his mug of tea. He was infused with interest as he got out of his side hatch, slopping the mug's contents when he slid down onto the ground. He came around Molly. 'Let's have a gander,' he asked, holding out his free hand for the binoculars.

'Between twelve and three o'clock from Mildred,' advised Meadows.

O'Hara lifted the optics to his eyes and scanned the area. He saw the strange assortment of *Volkssturm* troops immediately. 'Bloody hell, they do look like a bunch of old blokes. There're some young lads among them too – granddads and grandsons. They're definitely not regular soldiers, that's for sure. They're crawling under and over the broken trees. What on earth do the sneaky sods think they're doing? There's no attempt to hide from our observers.'

'I know,' replied Meadows. 'At first there was, but now they seem to have thrown caution to the wind. We could start selling tickets to watch the event.'

At that moment, Sergeant McGrew climbed back out of Molly holding a second pair of binoculars. He jumped down and returned with Louis following. The entire crew stood watching and waiting as they looked through the foliage.

'I've informed HQ. I think they already knew. Let's see if they do anything,' added McGrew.

'I reckon they're letting them fill the area up. Then we'll bombard it again – it'll be a question of the more, the merrier.' Meadows wore a look of displeasure as he spoke.

'Jerry high command must be ordering the poor sods in,' said Louis in a tone of sympathy.

'The poor sods don't realise what they're in for,' said McGrew sadly. 'They're probably looking at our three wrecks in the meadow and taking false heart from such a sight.'

They all jumped as the Allied guns let loose with a thunderous roar – a cacophony of wide-spreading booming sounds. More shells suddenly screamed across the basin.

'Holy shit!' muttered Meadows, putting his hands to his ears.

Everyone else squinted as the sky became alive with shrill whistles of shells passing overhead. Further gasps followed from the tank unit as explosions and fire erupted upon the already ruined position. A murderous brutality that disgusted the entire observation crew. They witnessed the horror show from the safety of their concealed position, each trooper hissing and wincing at the demeaning and diabolical sight. A dirty depravity that was very necessary to them, even though they were loathed and ashamed to admit it.

Youths and old men with no clue of what to do. Some vanished in an all-consuming upsurge of flame. Others were lifted and thrown through the air like rag dolls to smash back into the rumbling debris of quivering timber.

As the murderous bombardment continued, some wretched survivors desperately staggered out onto the open field towards the battalion's wrecked tanks. Anything to be away from the torturous cascade of flame coupled with flesh-and-bone-slicing shrapnel. An assortment of heavy machine-gun fire from all across the summit of the Allied lines began to spit flame from the upper woodlands with mortar bombs adding to the enhanced form of attack.

'Oh, my God!' Wingnut winced with sheer horror as he looked down into the basin where the helpless figures were cut down amid the intense surge of heavy machine-gun fire from multiple Allied positions. A powerful downpour of bullets striking among the panicking enemy troops. Wretched faces screaming in abject terror. Others fearfully watching the annihilation of those around. Petrified, knowing their turn was imminent.

Some of the *Volkssturm* troops reached the cover of the wrecked Sherman and the two Cromwell tanks but mortar shells were sporadically dropping about the wrecks.

The militia was being flushed out of the wrecked woodlands into the open to be scythed out of existence by the cold and cruel reality of a force desperate to win. A greater force determined to kill at any cost.

'Oh, bloody hell,' said Meadows. 'It's the law of things.'

'Aye,' muttered O'Hara. 'Kill or be killed.'

'Drink this harsh medicine, Wingnut. You have to,' said McGrew.

'This is the world we live in,' whispered Louis as he gritted his teeth. His eyes were watering with diabolical disgust. He had to remove his wet spectacles to clean them again.

CHAPTER 8

AN EERIE AND DIABOLICAL TRUCE

'Some of the poor bastards must still be alive down there,' muttered Louis. The entire aftermath was disturbing in a very different way to the explosive violence they had seen.

The bombardment had been over for about ten minutes and an eerie stillness settled over the basin. The tank crew continued to look down through the drifting smoke to the slaughter ground. Fires were burning all over the area – the battalion's three wrecked tanks were on fire again. Now there were countless bodies surrounding the burning wrecks – those of the *Volkssturm* militia lying strewn about. Many more dead would be in the newly pounded and burning woodlands.

'This is what our horrid shitshow is all about, Wingnut,' Sergeant McGrew muttered. 'You need to drink this reality in. War is a bloody messy business. There is nothing clean cut about it. This is our world and now it's yours too. You need to accept it if you want to stand a chance of surviving.'

'Those poor bastards didn't stand a chance,' said Wingnut. 'Why would Jerry send their own in there? They could see we have the high ground. They were just lambs to the slaughter.'

O'Hara sighed pitifully through his ugly broken nose, peering back at the young recruit from two black eyes. 'Welcome to the abattoir, Wingnut. You can be a lamb or a vegetarian slaughterman?'

'They are the only choices you have, by the way,' said Louis in support of his old friend.

'I understand what you mean. I will adapt and be that vegetarian slaughterman,' Wingnut replied. His face still remained calm and emotionless, but inside there was feeling. One only had to hear the recruit's questions to know there was a sense of feeling.

'You don't have to like what you do. It's a good thing, not to like it.' Louis tried to give Wingnut a little consolation.

'That little sum up with the vegetarian slaughterman was quite good for you, Billy O'Hara,' said Meadows. It was a comical dig but meant with a touch of decency.

O'Hara got out his pack of cigarettes and put one in his mouth before passing the pack around.

'I think we have to cling to the disgust. Even though we hate the shitshow, we have to go with the flow of it all and keep the disgust in tow. One day we'll stand before our maker and will have to atone for all of this. Every one of us. Even those poor bastards lying down there.'

'Just another episode of everyday life in the grand shitshow circus,' added Louis, lighting his cigarette.

Each trooper stood within the canopy of the overhanging holly bush and continued to observe the burning destruction. Here and there an injured soul tried to crawl.

'Some are still alive,' muttered Wingnut.

Meadows pointed to the south east. 'Look! A *Kübelwagen*. They're flying a white flag.'

The enemy vehicle sped over the rutted landscape towards the Allied area of ground. A large white sheet fluttered behind as the slight, yet robust-looking, vehicle's suspension lifted and lowered over the bumpy terrain. McGrew raised his binoculars and watched the approaching military car.

'There are two soldiers in the front,' said McGrew. 'An officer with an NCO driving. In the back are two civilians. One is a priest!'

'They want a truce to get their wounded out,' said Meadows.

'Now they want to appeal to our humanity,' added Louis.

'And we are expected to respond to theirs,' said O'Hara. 'I hope we do.'

'Then when it is all sorted, we can start killing one another again,' said Wingnut morosely.

'That's the way the biscuit breaks, lad.' McGrew lowered his binoculars. 'I bet God must think we're all a bunch of nit-twits.'

'I reckon he's looking down and laughing at us,' replied Meadows.

They watched as the German *Kübelwagen* dropped down into the narrow gully and drove through the little stream. Then it mounted up and out onto the Allied side and proceeded up the gentle rise of the hill towards the woodland where a line of weapons would be concealed and aiming at them in readiness.

'This lot have got some arsehole as well,' muttered Meadows admirably.

'You wouldn't catch me doing it, that's for sure,' O'Hara admitted.

They watched as the *Kübelwagen* drove past their hidden position about two hundred and fifty yards away. The entire tank crew hurried around Molly to the other end of the bush to continue watching the vehicle's climb. At some distance before the line of trees, the *Kübelwagen* braked to a halt with the big white sheet still fluttering rowdily from a pole at the rear of the vehicle. All four personnel got out of the car and raised their hands. They walked a few paces forward of the vehicle and stopped in a line.

Two Allied officers came out from the trees and approached the group. The priest and the German officer took two tentative paces forward, hands still raised.

McGrew spoke, 'That's Captain Dugard from the Canadian group and Captain Sedan from one of our artillery units.'

They observed as both Allied officers abruptly stopped and stood to attention. They respectfully saluted the German officer who smartly saluted back. Then they began to talk as the German officer appeared to introduce the priest.

'The parley begins,' said Louis. 'I'd love to hear what they're saying.'

'Probably getting straight to the point,' O'Hara suggested.

'If they get permission, they'll have to get a move on. It'll be getting dark in about another hour.' Meadows was looking into the grey overcast sky.

'Done and dusted!' said McGrew.

The two Allied officers saluted again and turned away. The officer and the priest looked back to their own lines and waved to and fro.

Déjà Vu McGrew and his Tank Crew

Once again, the tank crew went to the rear of Molly and watched things develop where the enemy lines and the carnage were. In the distance, two Red Cross trucks rumbled forward, followed by a couple of civilian cars. Then behind these came two horse-drawn carts.

'Blimey, they don't have many vehicles to use for the clear up,' said Wingnut. 'They're using horse-drawn carts.'

'The horse carts will suffice,' said Louis. 'They'll probably bundle the dead on there.'

Events quickly began to unfold as the observation group watched the entire drama. A work party of nurses and a few other medical orderlies quickly moved among the fallen *Volkssturm*. Each body was checked by a nurse before either a work party or another Red Cross orderly came forward. The prostrate figures retrieved by the work party were unceremoniously thrown onto the horse carts. Those checked by a medical orderly were put on stretchers and loaded aboard two ambulances. It was notable that most were loaded onto the horse carts. The entire event took between thirty and forty minutes before the vehicles and the horse carts moved away, and the whole process was watched in silence by the Molly tank crew.

As the sad affair was drawing to its conclusion, McGrew mumbled aloud, 'What a waste that little

Volkssturm escapade was. I wonder how many will survive?'

'They never bothered checking the slaughter in the woods,' said Wingnut.

'Anyone left alive in the woods will only get best wishes now,' said Meadows.

'I bet there'll still be a few regulars creeping in and hiding there once it gets dark,' said Louis. His war-seasoned fighting instinct was returning.

'You can bet on that one,' agreed Meadows.

'I reckon they still have a few eighty-eights and some other mounted guns. Maybe the odd tank. All of them lying in wait for us. Licking their lips for some payback, when we decide to do the next advance.'

'It'll be dark soon,' said McGrew. 'We better get blankets and other things prepared. We'll need to keep vigilant during the night. I wouldn't put it past Jerry to try something unexpected.'

'Not with *Volkssturm?*' Wingnut said.

'Not with *Volkssturm*, lad. Next time it'll be the big boys,' replied McGrew with a humorous smile.

Wingnut responded as his mood lightened. He nodded and replied, 'Back to the big boys next round, then.'

'You've already let them have a good taste of us, Wingnut, and you did well, lad. Bear that in mind too.' McGrew thought it important to praise the recruit. He deserved it.

This time Wingnut got out his cigarettes and took one before handing the pack to his sergeant. The pack was received with gratitude and passed around. The youngster was fitting in. Much to the superstitious dismay of the troop, they were all developing a liking for Wingnut. Just like the other troopers before him. The ones no longer alive.

McGrew spoke out to all, 'We'll finish these smokes and then get back inside Molly. Get the lanterns on and open the AFV and take some rations. It's been a challenging time today and maybe we could unwind a little before the night stint starts.'

'That sounds good to me,' Meadows agreed.

Louis nodded and smiled. 'I forgot all about eating during this testing day.'

'Testing and not eating is putting it mildly,' agreed O'Hara as he walked to the bush's interior layer and took one last look out at the basin before the dusk settled and obscured it all.

Wingnut retched as the putrid smell of flatulence caused his nostrils to flare and made him gag. 'Oh, what bastard done that?'

McGrew and Louis backed away from Wingnut with their faces twisted in disgust.

'Blimey, I think Wingnut just ate a slice of horrible shit. Who owns that one?' called Meadows in disgust.

'You can have it, if you want it,' grumbled Louis as he took a few steps back, holding his nose disapprovingly.

'God love us,' muttered McGrew. 'That's a blooming wicked one.'

'Who did that?' asked Meadows, looking at Wingnut.

'It's not me,' Wingnut protested, screwing his face up in distaste.

'Billy!' McGrew called angrily to O'Hara who remained silent, watching the basin in the settling dusk.

O'Hara turned to the group and nonchalantly replied, 'What?'

'Would that be one of yours? Would you have been dropping your guts again?' hissed McGrew.

O'Hara frowned thoughtfully and then answered, 'I might have done. I can't quite remember, that's for sure. But I might have done.'

'You dirty sod,' moaned Wingnut, who had taken the full force of the odious issue.

'You've got a dead rat up your arse,' complained Louis.

'That was a bit rich, Billy,' said Meadows with a slight note of awe. 'A good one, but a bit rich, mate, me old mucker.'

'That was a bit strong, Billy O'Hara,' continued McGrew. 'I can't understand how that stench got through one of these thick superbly lined pixie suits.'

Wingnut tried to embolden his disapproval. 'It's an armour-piercing—'

'Alright now, lads,' cut in McGrew. 'Let's be getting inside Molly and sorting out the AFV rations and the other provisions.'

'Can't Billy wait out here?' asked Meadows.

'Yes, perhaps that might be a good idea,' agreed McGrew. 'It gets a little cramped in there. You keep watch, O'Hara. I'll send something out.'

CHAPTER 9

THE NIGHT PARTY

It was pitch-black and very cold. Meadows and O'Hara stood watch. Both were eating from the donated supply of cakes and biscuits from appreciative liberated Dutch people. They also sipped at hot, sweet tea. The padded collars of their thickly lined pixie suits were turned up. The cap badges of their neatly fitting black berets rested above the left eye with the beret's drop to the right.

'Nice little add-on to our AFV pack.' O'Hara laughed appreciatively as he bit into his cinnamon cake.

Meadows replied, 'Lovely stuff! I think we all needed something. It's been a bastard of a day. We're all lucky to be here after that bloody encounter back there. We'll not be seeing Wilson anymore.'

'I thought the poor sod would get through the entire shitshow. One of the lucky ones,' added O'Hara, genuine in his reflection of the late trooper.

Meadows agreed and then continued, 'Lieutenant Samson never lasted long either. Nightingale had a better run than him.'

'I could see his card was marked from the word go. The bloke just had that look about him.' Then O'Hara looked back at Molly the tank to make sure no one was in earshot. 'Do you think Wingnut has the look of a poor sod?'

'Sadly, I do.' Meadows sighed unhappily. 'It's a pity because I rather like the lad. He's bloody good with Molly's gun. The old nag was on the move and he got those hits in good and proper. It was close range but he didn't panic. The lad was poetry in motion, Billy. The complete doggie's round ones.'

'That's high praise indeed,' muttered O'Hara. 'I thought he was good but I didn't see him in full action. I was blazing away about his strike areas. Got a few too, running about in the fire's glow. Yet you still don't think he'll get through the shitshow?'

'Honestly, Billy. I really hope I've got this wrong. I would give anything to be wrong, but I'm still having bad vibes about our new lad.'

'How do these bad vibes come?' asked O'Hara.

'Just thoughts, that's all. Thoughts of dread.'

'Sometimes, I wish you didn't keep getting this kiss-of-death feeling, Meadows. It really spooks me.' O'Hara popped the last part of his cake into his mouth.

'Does it? Do you put faith in my predictions?' Meadows laughed. 'I can be wrong, you know. Don't believe everything I predict. I do sometimes get it wrong. We actually indulge our superstitions. We are slavishly devoted to them in a way that's not always healthy.'

O'Hara had chewed and mushed his cake and then gulped it down. 'Well, I can think of four predictions after Caterpillar and Edwards.'

'Name them,' encouraged Meadows.

'Alonso, Sullivan, Fergusson and Parks. You said the same about them and each trooper fell. Your predictions are a bloody jinx. You also said we had auroras. Why can't Wingnut have one?'

'I don't get to decide about auroras, Billy. It's just old-fangled superstition, nothing more. It's spooky, but to be fair, I've said the dreaded thing about every new recruit that comes to us. It's part and parcel of the practice of prediction from me. You know that. Don't be letting it plague you too much. Don't be going all Irish and superstitious on me, Billy.'

'Well, I think there's something in it. Every recruit has got off this bus while on this shitshow route. You can't say it isn't true, now.'

Meadows sighed. He had become the creator of his own indulgent and whimsical speculation. He was very superstitious, but not like O'Hara. The man seemed to believe in his snatched-from-the-air predictions.

'All I'm trying to say, is that I like Wingnut. I've liked all of the lads. I wish there was something I could say or do that would help you believe that my predictions cannot always be true.' Meadows shook his head in amusement as he stared at O'Hara.

'You're a blooming jinx, John Meadows, that's for sure. Every time you predict, it comes true. Why not predict something good for our Wingnut? He's a good lad and I would like for him to have one of these auroras you've been dishing out.'

Meadows began to laugh at his long-time comrade. 'For Christ's sake, Billy. You're taking this way too seriously. Now you're spooking me. Let's be honest, it's coincidence. I don't get to dish out protective auroras on people.'

'Coincidence be damned. You can put the mockers on things and you can take the mockers off.' O'Hara's eyes were wide with conviction.

'How would you like me to take the mockers off Wingnut, Billy? How on earth do I do that?'

O'Hara grinned and replied, 'The same way as you put the mockers on – by predicting it. All you have to say is that you predict Wingnut will get through the shitshow. Have you ever thought about that?'

Meadows raised his eyes and took a deep breath, followed by a quick sip of his tea. 'What would you have me say? "I predict that Wingnut will make it to the last stop. See the whole shitshow out"?'

O'Hara grinned like an uneducated superstitious peasant from the Middle Ages and replied, 'Aye, that's for sure.'

'Alright then, Billy O'Hara – just for you. I predict that Wingnut will get through the entire shitshow. Hey! How about that, I feel good vibes for the lad already. It must be working.'

'Yeah, but maybe there will be payback for one of us. You know how such things work.' O'Hara's mind was working overtime. 'When you start messing with such mystical things.'

'Oh, stack me!' Meadows cussed. 'There's no pleasing some people. Look, Billy, let me answer for this if you say I can. It's not going to happen to you or any of the other lads. My predictions, I answer for them. Ruddy heck, Billy. You don't know if you want to crap or get a haircut.'

O'Hara went silent for a moment and gave the matter some consideration, then said, 'Alright, then.'

'Are you sure now, Billy.'
'Aye, that's for sure.'

'I've a feeling this cold winter night is going to blooming fly by,' Meadows gasped.

Inside Molly, Wingnut was leaning against one side of the turret wall and Sergeant McGrew was against the other side. Louis was in his driving compartment and all were wrapped in blankets and trying to sleep in the dismal candlelight emitting from the two small lanterns.

Wingnut cleared his throat and McGrew whispered to him, 'Are you awake, Wingnut?'

'Yeah, I can't sleep,' came the reply.

'Me neither,' said Louis.

'None of us can get any shut-eye,' added McGrew. 'I'm knackered, but I just can't sleep.'

'I think it might have something to do with our predicament,' suggested Wingnut.

'Really?' replied Louis sarcastically.

'Nothing gets past you, Wingnut,' said McGrew, chuckling.

'Sharp as a sponge,' said Louis with a giggle.

'Well, can't any of you guys rustle up a nice little anecdote for me? A peach of a true story from the past?' asked Wingnut enthusiastically. He liked to hear their past stories and had laughed over the past few days as he'd listened to such tales.

'Our Wingnut is a bit of a glutton for an anecdote,' said Louis, laughing.

'Not all of our stories are fun ones, Wingnut. You know that,' said McGrew.

'I do, Serge. But then again, they aren't all bad. You don't have to let me in on the bad things. What about a kindlier story? Perhaps something comical,' said Wingnut.

'What do you think, Louis? Can you rustle one up?' McGrew asked.

Louis sniggered. 'Not a personal comical one. Not at the moment. Though you could tell him about your trip to the dentist back in Libya – when you thought your luck had changed because you got away from the front line with all its shelling and stuff.'

'Oh yes.' McGrew laughed at the sheer memory of the incident. 'That was a little gem. Worthy of any pub-time chat. Also, the departure of Nuts and Bolts. Now there was a character to make one giggle. That is a fine story to tell.'

'Not an after-dinner one, though,' Louis giggled, 'especially with ladies present.'

'I'm all ears,' replied Wingnut and realised it wasn't the best thing to say to such rudely drawn men.

In unison, McGrew and Louis replied, 'You can say that again!' and fell about their sitting positions with laughter.

'Oh, how we roared,' said Wingnut without an ounce of emotion.

Déjà Vu McGrew and his Tank Crew

'Alright then, lads, here we go with Sergeant McGrew's dentist trip. It was back in Libya during the desert war with the Jerry and Eyetie. I had been getting this toothache and was wanting the thing sorted out. We were waiting on our new Lee, or the Grant tank to come, at the time – the one we would lose to a Sturmgeschütz. We were milling about in some trench system with the enemy slinging all sorts of shit at us. Then one day, during a bombardment, when we were all getting pissed off doing infantry things in these trenches, I gets a message in the form of a note. I had to report to a certain Army headquarters and medical centre which they said was thirty miles back from the lines. Well, as you can well imagine, I'm over the moon. I get to leave the front for a while. I can leave all this constant shelling and get the niggling toothache sorted. Nuts and Bolts was due to accompany me, on account that he had a toothache too.

'So, I needed no second invitation, lad. I'm off like a bloody rat up a drain pipe, that's for sure. There I am with my backpack and webbing, raring to go.

'I hop on a lorry with Nuts and Bolts for company. Both of us were very pleased to see the front falling away and retreating from view as our happy truck motored off along the long and bumpy desert road. Imagine my further delight when I was told the compound we were making for was not thirty but a full fifty miles away from the front line. The administrative clerk had made a mistake. The best mistake he could make, to my mind. I wasn't going to complain on that score. Gradually, the boom of the guns diminished and the hot desert sun was rather pleasant with the truck creating an acceptable breeze.

'I can remember Nuts and Bolts with his swollen abscess around his jaw. He was delighted to be away too. I can still see him in my mind's eye ranting, "For once the pen pusher's got it wrong. This time the mistake is better – do you hear? The balls-up is better forever." It was in his usual quickfire way, the bloke's words spewing out like machine-gun fire. Still, the grand old trooper was thrilled. We all were. We had a little sing-song along the way, as you do in such situations. All in all, we were very pleased with ourselves.

'Finally, we gets to this compound. A smashing building in the middle of nowhere with a perimeter wall, inside of which was a vehicle parking area. There was a number of empty trucks there and the driver said he believed there were a lot of soldiers waiting to see the doctors and dentists at this compound station. It had a couple of palm trees over in one corner. A little oasis to my mind and well away from the shell slinging.

'I jumped out along with Nuts and Bolts and the rest of the lads. They all went running in to get their turns as far up the line as possible. I was in no hurry at all. I wanted to be on the blooming arse end of the queue. The quicker you get seen, the quicker you get back to the lines with all the shell slinging.

'When I gets inside of the waiting room, it was organised chaos. I mean, there were people on all of the seats with others sitting against the wall. There were just two lavatories with a long queue for both. Now I wanted to take a dump badly and I didn't fancy the wait or going in the toilet after so many other squaddies had been in the shithouse before me. It was Nuts and Bolts who suggested I make use of the spade and head off for the palm trees at the compound's rear perimeter. There, I could dig myself an accommodating hole behind the cover of some wooden box containers that our Nuts and Bolts noticed were stored there. I had my pack and my mini spade. I was in no hurry to register, so I decided to take the advice of Nuts and Bolts. Off I went outside, to dig myself an obliging hole behind the storage boxes by the palm trees. There I could take a discreet dump out of harm's way. I go behind the said wooden storage boxes and proceed to dig myself a nice little hole. I drops my strides and squat there to do my business.

'I'm midway into my distracting call of convenience when I hear this rumble of several vehicles coming into the compound on the other side of the building, where our truck had parked next to the vehicles upon arrival. More arrivals was great – they could all register before me and I was fine with being at the back of the large queue. Then I realised it had gone awfully quiet. For a few minutes, I continued with my party act—'

'Bloody hell, Serge,' Wingnut laughed as he interrupted the story, 'I bet you don't get invited to many parties.'

'Correct, lad! Now I'll continue with my rum little ditty, if you don't mind? I had just finished and wiped my arse. I refilled my hole of practicality and buried all disposable and unwanted contents. I was all ready to walk back to the building when I stopped. Rather gobsmacked, I was forced to reconsider my actions. Suddenly it was shouting and mayhem before my very eyes.

'Lord love us, if I didn't see this big "bugger off" Jerry Panzer III tank inside our car park. It had one of those new big "bugger off" gun barrels. There were also a couple of half-tracks too, each carrying loads of bad-mannered Afrika Korps fellas running about the place with their machine guns screaming, "*Schnell, schnell!*" or words to that effect. To be honest, they were screaming out all manner of things in their Jerry lingo – things I couldn't understand as I'm sure you can imagine. I could make out *schnell* and the word *Tommy* but beyond that I couldn't understand a thing.

'All our lads were paraded outside of the building with their hands in the air and made to stand in a line. They had all brought their packs and webbing with them, holding them up and above their heads, their toothaches and other untreated ailments alongside, no doubt. I spotted Nuts and Bolts looking about the men. I think he was hoping to spot me. I began to wonder if the silly sod would turn and look behind to my position of concealment. Fortunately, Nuts and Bolts didn't give me away. The poor sod, along with the rest of the men, was about to take a long sabbatical. For Nuts and Bolts the war was over, but at least I hope he's in a prisoner-of-war camp somewhere, especially if it's an Italian one. They're meant to be rather nice with kind weather most of the year.

'One young Jerry hothead was screaming blue murder at our boys. He was trying to order them to drop their webbing but they seemed to be reluctant. I think they might have been pretending not to understand. Then the young Jerry starts screaming and hollering at them to drop their packs, but again, our boys were looking a bit dumb. Then out comes a Jerry stick grenade and the screaming little hothead makes to pull the cord and sling it into the line.

'Well, our boys quickly became enlightened as to the impolite request of their Jerry captors. Every knapsack and bit of webbing dropped like an entity of knowing discipline. It all hit the floor like a smash to attention. I bet our lads' various parade ground RSMs would have been proud of their response, that's for sure.'

Wingnut laughed and asked, 'Did they all get carted off?'

McGrew nodded. 'Every single one of them, even our Nuts and Bolts character. The doctors and the dentists too. It was just me behind the boxes and the palm trees. I sneaked over the perimeter wall and made off behind a nice big sand dune and sat there hoping they would all bugger off. Eventually, I heard the rumble of vehicles and when I dared to look back twenty minutes later, Jerry was gone with all our lads, our trucks, the Panzer III and the half-tracks. I couldn't believe what had happened. I was fifty miles within our lines. Jerry was meant to be that far away. But there they had been, as large as life and capturing a dentist and doctor's waiting room full of ailment-stricken soldiers secure in their ill-deserved confidence of time away from the front. Well, they all got a little more time away than they bargained for.'

'That was a shame. I missed our Nuts and Bolts. The prisoners would have been shipped out to Italy,' Louis commented. 'Remember those POWs we came across in Italy. The Eyeties let them all go just after Salerno.'

'What about them?' asked Wingnut.

McGrew laughed at Louis' recollection. 'They were pretty sore at us, if I remember.'

'Why?' Wingnut was confused.

'They thought Italy was nice,' Louis replied. 'The Italians were smashing hosts and the local village ladies used to come to the prison camp and do their washing and give them little bits of food. Your Eyeties were fairly decent to our captured blokes, according to the ones we met. When we liberated them, these ex-POW men had to return to fighting duties.'

'Aye,' agreed McGrew. 'They had gone soft, that's for sure. But Nuts and Bolts was never liberated or he would have come back to us, that's for sure.'

Louis chuckled some more. 'Maybe our Nuts and Bolts is further north in the Jerry-occupied part of Italy. Or he may have been transported into the Fatherland. He definitely is captured. We got word via the usual route.'

'What happened to you when the Jerries left the compound with all our lads as prisoners?'

'I hung around and wandered the compound for a bit, hoping that someone else may have had my luck and escaped capture. Then a couple of those long-range chevy vehicles come along with a few of our lads crammed inside. They were all wearing Arab headgear and had an assortment of strange weapons. They were some sort of shit-hot "don't mess with us" group.

'I told them what had happened and then they told me about this Jerry breakthrough along our lines. To the north there had been an attack and Jerry was sweeping south in a flanking movement. The compound was caught in the Jerry sweep and this ragtag, devil-may-care group of lads agreed to give me a lift. One bloke was a sort of medic and he sorted my tooth out while we were on the move.'

'We were all shocked to see Serge a few days later,' replied Louis.

McGrew grinned. 'I often wonder if those lads, captured at the compound, were as angry as the other POWs we liberated in Italy. I like to think they would have been a little more gracious. That's if they stopped in Italy. They might be in a POW camp in Germany.'

'We'll never know,' replied Wingnut, delighted with the story. 'That was a close shave, Serge. A very close shave, indeed.'

The cupola hatch opened from above and McGrew looked up to see O'Hara. 'What's up, Billy?'

O'Hara whispered, 'Meadows and I have heard voices in the darkness. It's not the breeze. They were definitely voices – Jerry voices, Serge.'

Everyone stood up, all anxious to investigate but all were cautious as well. Louis had grabbed a Sten sub-machine gun. Wingnut took one too.

The recruit then asked, 'Why have we got three Sten sub-machine guns?'

'We just acquired more along the way, Wingnut,' replied Louis.

McGrew whispered to them both, 'Do not fire unless I order. Have you got that, lads?'

'Yes, Serge,' each trooper replied in unison.

'Quiet as can be now, lads – dismount.'

Stealthily, each trooper emerged from Molly via their own hatches and gingerly climbed down to the cold earth beneath the canopy of their concealed position. It was almost pitch-black. The bitter cold air was refreshing and served to invigorate their alertness. Over by the rear of the cover, Meadows could be made out in the shafts of moonlight that broke through parts of the bracken. He had unslung his Sten gun and was holding it in readiness with one hand, his free hand signalling for the group to remain quiet. He turned his head slightly as he strained to listen.

McGrew gingerly moved to stand beside him and whispered, 'Have you heard anymore?'

'Yes, Serge. Listen.' He held up a finger and McGrew complied – straining to hear something.

There came the sound of faint voices. Far-off German chatter. It was definitely German people talking.

'I got that. What the hell are the bastards up to?' McGrew wondered.

'Probably a forward observation unit. They can't be in any vehicle. We would have heard it. But they are up to something and I would guess they have a radio and are reporting back, maybe preparing the way for one of their tanks or assault guns,' Meadows suggested.

'Oh Christ, not more of those bloody ambushing Sturmgeschütz things. We're going to have to do something if they are a forward unit for one of those things. They'll have a clear view over the pontoon bridge from that small cluster of trees – a few quick shots, then off before we can reply. This has been one heck of a bloody day and now we're in for a night of it too,' McGrew hissed as he turned to the others at the side of the tank. The gloom was so intense he couldn't make them out.

'O'Hara and Louis, look to the front of the cover,' he whispered into the pitch-black, and then added, 'Wingnut, come here.'

McGrew could only assume that O'Hara and Louis had made to the front of Molly and the covered entrance, though he never saw or heard them. Wingnut's hazy form in the padded pixie suit emerged from the black. The recruit was clasping his Sten gun with his jaw firmly set. He stopped before McGrew who turned and waved for him to come closer where he stood with Meadows. He was flummoxed, as though wondering how to handle the situation, and began to formulate his method as he went along. It was his usual way.

'Right, I and Wingnut will go and check this out. I want you to keep watch at this point and keep listening. The password will be pixie suits. Have you got that?'

'Yes,' replied Meadows, 'but why pixie suits?'

'Because I just said it was,' hissed McGrew.

'I just wondered what made you think of pixie suits,' Meadows whispered back.

'We're wearing them,' muttered Wingnut in reply.

'It doesn't bloody matter,' hissed McGrew under his breath. 'Why do you blooming English always have to make a pointless debate out of everything?'

'Are we going out there then, Serge?' Wingnut asked quietly.

'Yes, Wingnut. I just said that.' McGrew was becoming clearly irritated by the troopers. 'Why have you two slipped into that ruddy dimwit-gear?'

'We're in pixie suits?' Wingnut seemed confused.

McGrew tried to calm himself down and then held up a placating hand. 'Just shut the heck up. The pair of you! Wingnut, follow me.'

Wingnut complied and followed Sergeant McGrew into the gloom, back along the side of Molly and to the front of the cover where O'Hara and Louis were standing.

McGrew whispered his intentions. 'Wingnut and I are going to sneak out and take a look. The password is pixie suits, do you understand?'

'Why pixie suits?' asked O'Hara.

McGrew's jaw muscle strained as he tried to contain his irritation. 'Don't be going all bloody English on me, Billy. I couldn't be taking that.'

Wingnut tried to stay impassive and dared not snigger. Then he found the perfect excuse to take his mind from the comical banter. He screwed his face up and pressed his fingers to his nose and quietly mumbled, 'Have you done it again, O'Hara?'

'I didn't know you were coming back here. I thought it would be alright,' O'Hara whispered his rebuke.

'God love us,' hissed McGrew. 'Louis, the password is—'

'Pixie suits, Serge. Can't I come too?' whispered Louis, holding his nose.

McGrew caught the strong odious whiff of O'Hara's testing flatulence and his sympathy was won over. 'Alright, Louis, you can come too.'

He turned back to O'Hara and said, 'Stay at this end, Billy. Meadows is at the other and the password is?'

'Pixie suits, Serge,' answered O'Hara, looking sheepish in the moonlight.

CHAPTER 10

THE SMALL OBSERVATION UNIT

The cold night was helpful as McGrew furtively led his two troopers across the frosty earth, hugging every dip and edging closer in the direction where he suspected the chatter had come from. Far off, to the south, the sound of guns rumbled like distant thunder. Then it began to lightly rain.

'Almost like the threat of an approaching storm,' whispered the cautious sergeant.

Louis edged to the side of McGrew and replied with equally hushed tones, 'It might be of help to us, Serge.'

Wingnut was close behind, following every move and hiding behind every bit of cover. Like the others, he was looking around the surrounding area and trying to make out anything recognisable. He and Louis clutched their Sten sub-machine guns while McGrew held his Enfield revolver at the ready.

The dim forms of tree trunks became apparent amid hazy, spitting rain. They were bathed in a cloud break of gloomy moonlight. The troopers crept closer to where they knew the enemy voices had come from, each man's vision cautiously examining the trees.

McGrew signalled for Louis and Wingnut to stay put and then dashed over to one of the tree trunks at the wood's perimeter. He turned back and held up one finger and beckoned. Wingnut dashed across the open ground, crouching as he made for a tree to stand beside McGrew.

'Hide by that next tree there, lad. Fan out a little,' whispered McGrew.

Wingnut crouched again and dashed across to another tree's cover. He turned and watched as McGrew beckoned for Louis to come across the open ground. Quickly and silently, Louis made the run, crouching low like Wingnut. He then went a couple of trees down along the other side of Sergeant McGrew. Each trooper had his own slice of cover with McGrew in the middle. He signalled again for each of them to sneak forward. They both complied and moved deeper into the dark wood. The spitting rain lessened to a greater degree amid the trees, almost unnoticeable. The night was still very cold but each trooper was perspiring with fear as he went deeper into the dark abode bathed in shards of eerie moonlight.

Then they froze in unison. The sound had carried on the light breeze. They heard the low-key chatter of voices. Louis and Wingnut looked to McGrew for instruction. He lowered to a crouching position and signalled for them to do likewise.

The chatter was quiet but evident – something the group didn't expect. The people were very close. In that sense, it was careless. It surprised McGrew.

Unusual for Jerry, he thought to himself. *Perhaps recruits trying to do a more senior soldier's work?*

Wingnut peered into the gloom and made out the ghostly form of an enemy soldier in the scattered mist. The human shape was thickly padded in a large overcoat with the ominous outline of the standard German helmet. His eyes adjusted and he was able to focus upon a second figure – the same type of overcoat but wearing the field cap. He looked sideways to McGrew and pointed to his eye then held two fingers up and pointed towards the ghostly apparitions through the trees.

McGrew followed his line and caught sight of the men. As he scrutinised, he made out a third figure and turned back to Wingnut who was holding up three fingers. He had seen the third figure too and was correcting his information.

McGrew signalled for each trooper to crawl. Again, they complied. Slowly, each trooper carefully edged forward through the cold forest ferns and across the rock-hard sod. Their best source of concealment was the fog. The low-key voices became more distinguishable and Wingnut caught a few words he recognised as they gingerly edged closer through the ferns and around the covering trees.

'*Wir werden eine klare Schusslinie an der Zufahrtsstraße haben,*' he heard a voice say.

Something to do with a clear line of fire. Of this, Wingnut was certain. He strained and smiled to himself. He wanted to inform McGrew but was unable to at such a distance without alerting the enemy. He would wait until they were back or closer to whisper. He continued to crawl forward and saw that McGrew was doing the same thing to his right. Louis would be further to McGrew's right.

Then Wingnut tensed again. He heard a faint radio crackle and caught further hissed and desperate words. Most were unrecognisable, but he did catch the words sounding like, '*Verspottender Vogel, verspottender Vogel. Herein kommen.*' He assumed it was a radio call and something to do with a type of bird. Perhaps a contact name.

The fear was gripping but something emboldened each man to push on. Louis could make out each enemy soldier clearer now. He was on his stomach peering through a fern. The enemy chatter was almost shameful. They were whispering but could clearly be heard on the night air. The

Germans obviously knew their enemy was up on the bluff within the main treeline, but surely they should have been alert to observation units, like Molly's tank crew, hiding along the scarp. Perhaps the enemy had decided their small grove within the woods was the best place. They seemed secure in ill-deserved confidence that no Allied forces were hiding in such an obvious position. That had to be the reason – it was too obvious. Why did the Germans not realise this and deduce the Allies might hide somewhere else? There were three of them – older-looking men of the *Volkssturm*. The new shape of things to come for the Allied forces. The national militia comprised old veterans and youths. These older men were a mishmash group – brave, but inexperienced. They must have seen the slaughter of their comrades earlier in the evening. Yet still, they had the courage to take incredible risks.

The radio set crackled again and one of the old soldiers began to speak into it. '*Verspottender Vogel, verspottender Vogel. Herein kommen.*'

A silence followed and then the old soldier replied, '*Eine klare Schusslinie zur Zufahrtsstraße auf der anderen Seite des Flusses.*'

Another moment of silence while the radio operator listened to his headphones.

'*Ich verstehe. Wir werden auf weitere Anweisungen warten.*'

Then it happened. One of the other enemy soldiers stood up and muttered, '*Ich muss mal pissen.*'

The soldier's moonlit outline broke away and came towards the wooded area where McGrew and his men lay in hiding. The enemy's shape wore a long, thick, puffed-out overcoat. His field cap had been unbuttoned over the peak to allow the flaps to hang down the side of his head as ear protection against the cold night. The shadowed form ambled closer to where Louis was lying prostrate on his stomach beside a tree.

The soldier stopped at a tree close to the position where Louis was concealed. The unknown man undid his great baggy coat and then his trousers, cleared his throat and began to nonchalantly urinate against the tree trunk. For those few seconds, the shadow was preoccupied with his minor endeavour and suspected nothing. He looked up through the trees at the half-moon and shivered. The drizzle had stopped. So had the distant guns. There was only the sound of his passing water. An old soldier lost in his relief and sure, in the misguided knowledge, of being obscured from enemy sight.

Louis raised himself up against the cover of the silver birch next to the preoccupied figure. The trooper withdrew his knife – a weapon he had been trained to use on many an exercise, a situation he had re-enacted before upon an acting sentry. It was stealth and practice play with a knife. He knew how to grab the unsuspecting target and how to slide the blade in beneath the base of the skull upwards. But it was only theory and training practice. Louis had never put such training to the test. He never seriously believed he would have to. But now, something gripped his reason and his shadow showed the body language of resolve and commitment. Now it was for real. Make use of the training and put it into appropriate practice. This time it would result in murder in all but name. Dispatch – kill or be killed.

McGrew watched on in stunned silence as his eyes widened with dread. He had gulped fearfully as Louis' shadow stood up beside the tree. He knew his driver was going to make the killing move.

My God, he's going for it! thought the veteran sergeant as he continued to watch the event unfold.

Amid the shafts of moonlight, McGrew and Wingnut watched their fellow trooper's outline move rapidly forward to the tree where the German soldier was urinating. There was not a sound, just the impression of someone momentarily shocked. A wretched figure with no time to react as the silent but brief confrontation disappeared behind the misty trees. Then they saw Louis' moon-bathed shadow move backwards, clasping the jerking profile of the unknown enemy soldier. It was like watching a stage play of silhouettes, and they noted the spasmodic jerking of the victim's leg. Then the stillness of the enemy soldier's body as Louis gently laid the dead man down near to the close chatter of his unaware comrades.

McGrew gave Louis the thumbs up. However, it meant the other two would need to be dealt with. Why the enemy soldiers had chanced such a move to the wood was beyond the sergeant. All he could fathom was that they were an observation unit and they had a radio. Did they have a vehicle hidden somewhere? Were there more of them?

Wingnut had crawled over to him. He seemed to know something and McGrew decided to indulge the lad.

In a hushed whisper and behind a tree trunk Wingnut whispered, 'They're speaking of a clear line of fire. I think they mean the approach road across the main river. The ground dips down steeply beyond the glade, almost like a little cliff edge on this side of the river. As you know, it overlooks the approach road on the opposite bank.'

'It must be a recce for one of their big guns to do a hit and run,' McGrew whispered back. 'That would make sense. But how the hell could they get a Tiger or a Sturmgeschütz up here without making a noise?'

'They must have come up during the night. Probably on foot,' replied Wingnut.

'Aye, lad,' agreed McGrew. 'We'll have to take the other two.'

The seasoned sergeant looked over to Louis. He could just make him out, standing behind the tree where he had emerged to kill the enemy soldier.

McGrew held up his two fingers for the remaining soldiers and then ran his finger across his neck. The other two would need to be dispatched. Louis nodded his recognition and stayed put. He made some hand signals that McGrew understood.

'Soon one or both of the other enemy soldiers will come to check out their friend's absence. Now we have the growing tension of waiting,' whispered Wingnut, clearly becoming more anxious.

'Louis has just signalled that too. Wingnut, you remain here and shoot any of the sods that break to run. Louis and I will try to take them silently, but you keep watch over the events, do you understand, lad?'

'Yes, Serge,' replied Wingnut.

'Good lad, don't let us down, now. Keep watch and act only if necessary.'

'I will, Serge.'

McGrew began to crawl around the other side of the two German soldiers.

Louis remained standing behind his tree, watching over the corpse of his recent kill. Then Wingnut had to stop himself gasping out in surprise as he watched Louis gingerly lower himself onto his knees. He continued to observe with mounting awe as the driver's shadow stretched out from beyond the tree cover to pick up the dead soldier's field cap. It was an afterthought of preparation and Wingnut realised what Louis was trying to do. The shadowy figure in the thickly lined pixie suit stood up and removed his beret to replace the headwear with the German field cap.

Clever, clever, thought Wingnut.

The German soldier was wearing a thick padded coat and within the dark of the glade, the outline of the enemy cap would buy a few split seconds of expected familiarity before being recognised.

When Wingnut turned to whisper to McGrew, he was shocked to see that the sergeant had stealthily crawled off towards the two remaining enemy soldiers. They were knelt by their small radio set that was against the mud wall of an embankment. It gave McGrew more opportunity to circle around and approach from above the frozen earth wall where the two enemy soldiers were knelt below.

Then it happened! Wingnut tensed as he made out the chatter of the remaining comrades. '*Ich dachte Peter würde pissen, nicht scheißen.*'

One of the German soldiers stood and picked up a Schmeisser MP 40 machine gun and walked towards their position. He quietly hissed, '*Peter, was machst du?*'

Wingnut looked to Louis' hidden form and saw the trooper had his knife ready, yet the unseasoned recruit felt his heart thumping at the sight of the well-known enemy Schmeisser. He readied his Sten machine gun and pointed it at the advancing German. He wanted to fire, but instead, gritted his teeth. He silently scolded himself, *Wait! Not yet!*

The recruit continued to watch the nerve-wracking drama unfold. The enemy soldier hissed again. '*Wisch deinen verdammten Arsch ab und verschwinde von hier.*'

The enemy soldier took a few steps forward and saw Louis' shadow in Peter's familiar peak cap. Making as though to stand from his crouching business of defecation and adjusting his clothing, Louis showed the advancing German what he wanted to see – an image that looked like his friend in the misty woods.

Wingnut relaxed his finger that was about to fire his Sten gun. It was a relief to hear the dismissive and relaxed tone of the enemy soldier as he said, '*Bist du fertig?*'

Then Wingnut watched the new development of the dreadful drama as the German soldier turned to go back – momentarily satisfied by the sight of his perceived friend Peter. Such short-lived ease abruptly ended when the man gulped in astonishment. Instead of his friend being by the radio set, he looked into another pair of hard, cruel eyes, those belonging to a British trooper in a padded tank uniform and a black beret – an enemy trooper staring up at him from the embankment. He was holding down his comrade – firmly restraining the old radio operator around the neck with one arm. The British sergeant's other hand was behind his friend's neck. The assailant held something firmly to the base of his comrade's skull and was wriggling and twisting the implement with accepted and disgusted conviction while staring back at the surprised and alarmed soldier. The startled enemy soldier's mouth fell open in horror as he realised the radio operator was all but dead. Before him, he saw the gritted teeth of the British assailant as he stared back, an evil and wicked glint in ice-cold, cruel blue eyes.

From his hidden position, Wingnut felt a brief pang of pathetic sympathy. He heard the frightened soldier say, 'Joachim!' The remaining enemy soldier knew his friend was dead. The man was confused, his wits suddenly scrambled, was about to call and warn Peter. But unbeknown to him Peter was dead too. He thought Peter was about to stand beside him as he lifted his MP 40 machine gun. But he was further shocked to see a black man wearing Peter's cap.

Wingnut knew Louis must have observed the German soldier's wide eyes as well. The knife was already in the soft tissue of the shocked man's throat. Louis grabbed the Schmeisser with his free hand and locked his leg around the foe's leg. He tripped the soldier backwards onto the frozen woodland floor and both vanished under the layer of freezing mist.

There followed the sound of hideous choking gurgles and a muffled grunt of terrified protest. Wingnut watched in shocked awe as the woodland mist obscured Louis and his victim. Then the recruit was relieved when Louis stood up through the mist a few seconds later. He was clutching the prized German MP 40 machine gun.

It was over – three German observers were dead and all three British troopers gathered around the small radio the Germans had been using.

'Drag the bodies back here by the radio,' commanded McGrew.

Wingnut went to Louis' first victim while Louis dragged the recently killed soldier to lie with his comrade dispatched by Sergeant McGrew. Eventually, Wingnut had dragged the first victim to the embankment wall too. All three enemy soldiers lay dead by their radio set while Louis was looking at his newly acquired MP 40 Schmeisser. 'I've always wanted to get me one of these things. Are there magazines down there among their stuff? They must have…'

Sergeant McGrew lifted the belt containing the replaceable magazines. 'Enjoy the thing while the ammo clips last,' he said with good humour.

Louis smiled and replied, 'Thanks,' and took the magazine satchel.

Wingnut was retrieving a Luger pistol and some ammo clips. He looked up and asked, 'Can I take this?'

'Take what you can carry,' replied McGrew as he started to search the dead men's things.

The search was brief and there were a few things taken for personnel use, including two Mauser rifles. By far, Louis seemed the most satisfied with his MP 40 machine gun. He had a beaming smile as he shouldered his prize and gripped his Sten gun.

'I'll keep the Schmeisser as a spare,' he whispered.

'I want us to go further to the end of this wood. Where it looks out over the river,' muttered McGrew.

All three moved on, but there was hardly much distance to cover. Within less than a minute of stealthily moving through the trees, they came to the end of the small woods to a steep gradient of open land leading down to the flowing river. It could almost have been a cliff edge. The half-moon was still shining through a cloud gap in the night sky. The men looked about for a while and then all three turned their attention to the rough path leading eastwards and down. Down towards the enemy position where there had been some fierce fighting during the day. There was a small raised embankment that hid a ledged approach upwards to their position and along the river.

'A ledge big enough for the group of observers to use under cover of night. Also, big enough for a vehicle,' suggested Wingnut.

'They never used any form of transport,' said McGrew.

Louis agreed with McGrew's speculation. 'It would make too much noise in the night. One flare, and they'd be seen by all.'

'I don't think there are any others in the wood,' whispered Wingnut. 'But the blokes you killed were definitely talking about the approach road. The one on the other side of the river, I think. I'm certain I understood that part correctly. They were also calling something that sounded like a type of bird over the radio.'

'Probably a code name for the receivers,' whispered Louis, looking about at the eerie setting.

'And sooner or later they will wonder what happened to their brave blue-eyed boys,' murmured McGrew, looking down the approach path.

Wingnut wanted to emphasise his point. 'They must have crept up along the incline when it got dark. Any of our observers would have seen them in daylight, especially on the other side of the river. They would have been exposed. But during the night, they could get up unobserved. I doubt they have been here as long as us. They clearly had no knowledge of our presence.'

'We need another little bombardment with a couple of stray shells dropping on this wooded position,' said McGrew.

Louis nodded and smiled at the sergeant's line of thought. 'That would give us the excuse we need for Jerry to suppose their little observation unit got killed in an artillery barrage. When they try to call in, over the radio, they'll think a shell took them. It's better they deduce that than assume there is a small group of us lads close by.'

McGrew nodded and replied, 'We'll get back and call HQ from Molly. I'm sure we can work something out.'

'They might have been preparing the area for something to have a go at the approach road across the river. They definitely seemed interested in that, if what I could understand was correct.'

'It makes sense,' agreed McGrew. 'But in the meantime, we need to get a new bombardment going back down in the gully with a few strays to land in this wood.'

'Another bombardment,' Wingnut said. Then added, 'Just for a change.'

Louis agreed. 'It would give Jerry a good reason to suppose their lads were lost by a few stray shells.'

Wingnut nodded. There was merit in such a thing and the troop were experienced in such matters. More so than he was.

CHAPTER 11

ANOTHER BOMBARDMENT

Meadows had gone inside Molly the tank to watch and listen to McGrew's radio call back to Squadron HQ. He put the water on to boil for tea and was shocked by the tale of the German observation unit being in the nearby woods. He had the loader's hatch open and could hear the whispered excitement about the encounter. The cover of the natural lair offered some protection against the winter night's cold breeze and being inside Molly with the water boiling was an added extra. As the water boiled, he couldn't resist standing for a quick check of the radio valve settings. All seemed fine. He gave the sergeant a thumbs up and returned his attention to the stove.

Outside the tank, but under the bush's canopy, O'Hara was voicing his awe and delight of Louis' captured MP 40 machine gun.

'That's a right good-looking piece of work, that is,' he muttered. 'I've always wanted one of those things, that's for sure.'

'Yeah, well this one is mine, Billy. I've always liked these Jerry machine guns. They look the doggies' big ones.' Louis was showing off his prize.

'I'll give yer ten bob for it,' said O'Hara.

Meadows popped his head out of his hatch and looked down at O'Hara. 'I already offered him two pound ten and he told me to go forth and multiply.'

'That's a splendidly polite way of saying it to avoid the F word,' said Wingnut with a grin, impressed with the troop's creative sayings to avoid the puritanical wrath of Sergeant McGrew.

'You turned down two pounds ten shillings?' O'Hara looked shocked. 'How much are you after, then?'

'I'm not selling, Billy,' Louis replied. 'I've told you already. This is mine. I've always wanted a Jerry machine gun.'

O'Hara was full of envy and stared at it. 'How did you get yourself that?'

'Louis took a Jerry down who was about to use it on Sergeant McGrew,' Wingnut answered nervously. 'He did a right old number on two Jerries.'

O'Hara looked at Wingnut. The lad had said it with a tense agitation. The whole affair had been exciting at the time. Now he was crashing out of the recollection and viewing the event from a different perspective. He meant well, but he was a recruit and it was an up-close and a first face-to-face personal encounter. The tank action earlier during the day had also begun to make its mark.

'Are you alright, Wingnut? Are you coming down a bit too quick? It's alright, mate. It happens. The shock after the adrenalin rush.'

Wingnut began to shake a little as he nodded and smiled. 'I think so.'

'Give him a fag, will ya?' O'Hara had run out and his spare packs were inside Molly.

Louis got his pack out and told Wingnut to move to the side of the tank and sit down. The recruit complied as Louis and O'Hara joined him, sitting on the cold earth beneath the overhang of the wild holly bush. He accepted the cigarette that Louis offered.

'Thanks,' he said and leaned forward to accept the light. The giant shrub's bowl-shaped dip hid them from view and so did the tank's cover.

Wingnut blew out a satisfying stream of smoke as Meadows, who had dropped back inside his loader's hatch, re-emerged holding some hot tea which he was silently stirring some powdered milk into.

'Sorry, there's no sugar, Wingnut,' whispered his loader.

'Ta.' Wingnut smiled as O'Hara reached up and took the cup. He handed it down to the youngster.

Meadows winked at O'Hara and Louis. 'I'm just doing you lads a brew too. Back in a jiffy.' He went back inside the hatch.

McGrew was talking in his usual radio jargon and obviously listening via his headphones. The words often seemed to be an innuendo of things easily understood, yet it was hard to know what appraisal was coming back without hearing the reply. That was for Sergeant McGrew through the headphones. The rest of the tank crew would have to wait until their tank commander had finished. Then all would be told of the outcome concerning McGrew's report to Squadron HQ.

Hot water on their mini stove boiled again and the metal teapot received the boiling contents upon soggy tea leaves reused for a second time. Four more tin mugs waited to be filled with powdered milk at the ready. As Meadows completed the minor chore, he placed one tin mug on the radio bracket, gesticulating to McGrew that it was his. The sergeant gave a thumbs up in appreciation as he continued his radio chatter about a suggested bombardment of the wood close by.

Once through his hatch, Meadows leaned down and handed two more hot mugs to O'Hara. The little Irishman gave one to Louis and kept one for himself. Meadows then climbed down from the hatch with his own tin mug of piping hot tea and squatted beside the others, and gratefully accepted a cigarette from Louis.

'Well, isn't this all cosy and nice,' whispered Meadows jokingly as he shivered in the night's cold. 'Hopefully the top brass will be sending over some more shit close by. Close enough to keep us bloody warm.'

'Not too close, I hope.' O'Hara looked a little nervous.

Louis had his German machine gun lying across his lap, his tea in one hand and his cigarette in the other. 'It will have a few dropping a bit close for comfort, but I think the closeness and the grid references are within artillery specs to score direct hits. I bloody hope so anyway.'

'That doesn't exactly fill me with confidence,' replied Meadows. 'What do you say, Wingnut?'

'I'm with you on the confidence front, but I also think our boys can pull the woods off. We are close. Hopefully hitting a fat tart's arse with a banjo type of close.' Wingnut smiled, glad to return Meadows' old saying.

Meadows smiled back. 'Let's hope so, me old mucker. Or it's liable to turn into a rather disappointing night.'

'More fireworks, aye?' Louis laughed.

There followed some nervous tittering about the expected event and the group of tank men huddled together in the coldness of the winter night. Their pixie suits did much to stop the biting cold and the cover of the holly and the overhang stopped the chill breeze getting directly to them. Their sunken hideaway did offer splendid protection.

McGrew climbed out of his cupola and stood on the hull looking down, his form just about recognisable as shafts of moonlight broke through the leafy canopy.

'We have about ten minutes, lads. I think we had all better mount our Molly mare while this is going on. There'll be a lot of light and we'll need to be vigilant and keep watch from inside the tank, now. Finish your tea and come inside.'

'That suits me fine,' said O'Hara with the same moonlight sheen bathing his toothless grin, broken nose and two black eyes.

'You look like you've done twelve rounds with Jock McAvoy,' said Meadows, laughing.

'He wouldn't last twelve rounds with me,' boasted O'Hara jokingly.

There followed some restrained giggling. O'Hara was a brawler and often got himself into scraps when on leave. Sergeant McGrew often referred to him as the silver medallist, yet it never stopped his enthusiasm.

'You know, Billy O'Hara,' muttered Meadows. 'I reckon if Jock McAvoy offered you an upfront go in the ring, you would go for it, wouldn't you?'

'Oh, I'd do it for the crack. Who could turn down such an opportunity?' O'Hara's black-ringed eyes were wide with boyish desire.

'You know, O'Hara,' said Louis. 'Sometimes I don't think you're the full shilling.'

This time O'Hara giggled. 'Have you only just worked that one out now, Louis? The rest have known since day one, now, that's for sure.'

Louis' huge white teeth glowed in the night and he held the German Schmeisser out to him. 'It's yours!' He grinned at his old friend. 'I wouldn't know what to do with it.'

O'Hara's eyes lit up and he grabbed the machine gun quickly, fearing Louis might change his mind. 'My God, are you sure, now, Louis? I've always wanted one of these. I thank you kindly for that, that's for sure.'

'No problem, mate,' replied Louis.

They all quietly chuckled. The camaraderie of close friends. It wasn't lost on Wingnut. The new recruit realised that some such deceased friends would have been bound to them in the same way. They had passed on. Killed in battle over a four-year stretch. He began to realise that these rudely drawn men were very fine troopers – very fine indeed.

They all put out the cigarette butts and stood up, casting the dregs of their tea over the hard soil. Then they all clambered onto Molly's hull, Louis and O'Hara using their hatch entrances while Wingnut and Meadows dropped in via the loader's hatch. McGrew went in via his cupola and closed the doors.

'Close all the hatch doors, lads,' McGrew said as he checked his watch. The tank's familiar confined space settling as each trooper took his position. The two candlelit lanterns threw a dim light upon the dirty gloss white walls.

'How long now, Serge,' asked O'Hara.

'Just reaching six minutes now, Billy,' McGrew replied.

'And what is this in aid of?' asked Meadows.

McGrew was turning his commander's periscope sideways. The explosions would light up on the wood close to them. The very wood visited by himself, Louis and Wingnut. An area where a dead enemy observation unit lay. He wanted to watch the explosions they all knew were coming.

'They'll bombard the lower basin area again,' he continued. 'Just to keep the enemy wary of putting more soldiers back. I think our lads mean to advance in the morning or sometime tomorrow. I also think they want to approach the Reichswald forest region or something like that. During this bombardment, they'll put a few stray shells in the

Déjà Vu McGrew and his Tank Crew

wood close by. This is so Jerry's lower observers can see their sneaky forward observation post, the one we have disposed of, getting blown up. Then Jerry might assume that's the reason for no radio reply.'

'Hopefully, Jerry assumes this?' Louis grinned.

McGrew took his face away from the periscope and looked over the breech towards Louis' driving compartment. 'That's the hundred-pound question. Will Jerry buy it?'

'I think they will, but they might still send someone up to look,' said Wingnut.

'They may do,' agreed McGrew. 'But we'll remain vigilant from here.'

'We can't hear much inside Molly,' said O'Hara, looking at his prized machine gun. It was cradled in his lap.

'No, but then we'll not hear much during a bombardment anyway. When it stops, we can get out and strain our ears.'

The small talk went on for a short time and various little issues were discussed about an advance on the Reichswald area, a place that no one seemed to know much about. McGrew had picked up on the area during the morning briefing, before the troop had gone on their ill-attempted patrol with the Firefly.

The first shells fired and took everyone by surprise, even though they knew it was going to happen.

McGrew looked through his periscope and the others used their various view ports. No one was interested in the lower basin that had been hit several times during the day and where the main emphasis of the bombardment was taking place. The tank's crew were only interested in the wooded area to the side of their hideout.

After the first minute, a stray explosion erupted within the woods and lit up the area with a glowing fire. Then two more shells landed within the woods.

'That's my boy,' yelled O'Hara, watching through his scope.

'I hope the Jerry observers below are gobbling this little lot up,' said Louis.

'Looks good to me,' replied Meadows. 'If I was a Jerry, I'd go for it.'

'Does it really matter if they do or don't?' Wingnut asked.

'Of course,' said Meadows. 'If Jerry knows his blokes were killed by Tommy sneaking about, Jerry might presume we're sneaking about around here. Which we are. And then, they might target our nice little hideaway. Being camouflaged and concealed only works if you don't give Jerry a reason to suspect your presence. Killing their blokes gives them some reason, unless we can fool them into thinking it was during a bombardment. They have probably been trying to contact them, but observers go silent on the radio for periods of time anyway. They wouldn't suspect anything unless it was prolonged. Now they have something prolonged – their blokes have been killed in the bombardment.'

Wingnut raised an eyebrow. 'Why not just radio for the bombardment without us going in for that risky close-quarter kill?'

'Because it's possible the Jerry observer unit could dodge the shells and survive a bombardment,' Meadows gasped. 'Bloody hell, Wingnut. Sometimes you can be blooming hard work.'

'I didn't think of that,' Wingnut replied sheepishly.

All continued to watch through the various viewer scopes as a fourth shell landed in the burning woods, the explosion slinging debris about as more flame lit the entire area. A sight to behold and Wingnut did think that any enemy observer who knew of the small observer post would be convinced of the unit's death during a bombardment.

'I have thought of one thing,' said Wingnut.

'Really,' said McGrew, deciding to indulge the recruit. 'What might that be, Wingnut?'

'If I was Jerry, I might use the noise to let a Sturmgeschütz or Tiger move up the path – that recessed pathway that we were looking at before we came back. The noise of the tracks and the engine would be drowned out in this bombing.'

McGrew looked impressed. 'That isn't bad thinking there, Wingnut. But it's highly unlikely. Also, the fires and explosions could shed light on any vehicle's advance.'

'Our Wingnut is a bit of a thinker,' suggested Meadows.

'That's not a bad thing,' muttered McGrew, intent on his periscope. 'The woods are burning away nicely. The whole area is lit up.'

No more shells fell on the burning woods. The fires lasted for some time and the shelling continued for about half an hour. By the time it came to a halt, each member of the tank crew was seated except for Sergeant McGrew. He was sitting on the turret floor with his legs outstretched.

'Well, that little barrage is over and if anyone can nab some sleep then I would advise you to try. I'll keep a look out. Good luck with sleep.' McGrew laughed.

'It's not the type of place I can grab some shut-eye,' Wingnut answered. 'This day will live with me forever. My first experience of action. The firefight this afternoon and then the killing in the woods. How many times have you blokes come this close?'

'Quite a few times, Wingnut,' replied Meadows. 'The three times we were unhorsed from tanks would be the most nerve-wracking. We've had plenty of scraps over three major campaigns but most were not as close as this. You don't get things like this happening too regular.'

Wingnut seemed to harbour a dreadful awe of the crew. 'The deserts of Africa, Italy and now across Europe. You blokes have been doing this sort of thing for four years and more.'

'Not day in and day out, lad. And this type of encounter is not always the place you could get killed in,' added Louis. 'Young Impett springs to mind. Do you remember that lad? That was back in North Africa.'

The rest of the crew nodded and O'Hara spoke, 'Oh Christ, yes. Young Impett. That was a poor little sod, that was for sure.'

Meadows nodded. 'Impett survived a lot of scraps too. He was a good trooper. He got the Panzer III that time. Took the thing out good and proper.'

McGrew frowned. 'I thought it was the Panzer IV. We got the III in Tunisia. Impett was already dead when we were in Tunisia.'

Meadows was pulling out his cigarette pack and he stopped and thought for a second. 'That's right, we got the Panzer IV first. In Libya. Impett got that one, side-on, as it came past the sand dunes. Two shots. One hitting the turret. Billy shot up Jerry as they bailed out. Not one prisoner out of that tank.'

'There was a lot going on that day, let's be honest,' said O'Hara. 'There was a lot of heavy fighting. That was a full-on day if ever I could remember.'

'You could have taken them prisoner because the battle literally stopped after Impett took out that Panzer IV,' said Louis. 'Not that any of us knew at the time. The fighting sort of thundered to a sudden halt when that tank got hit. The Jerries bailing out were just unlucky.'

'Oh aye,' agreed O'Hara. 'If I would have known that was the last bit of action for the day, I would have taken them prisoner. We just didn't know that Jerry was running out of fight.'

McGrew raised an enquiring eyebrow. 'You've never seemed too keen on taking prisoners, Billy. If none of us are to hand, you always seem to finish them off.'

'I don't like being burdened with prisoners during the height of a battle. I want to get the bastards out of the way. I took those two Italian artillery men prisoners when they hit your Matilda.'

'You brought them back and were about to machine gun them down in front of us,' said Meadows sarcastically.

'That was when I found out they had killed young Edwards. I was angry and would have done for them had the sergeant not stopped me.'

'That is true,' said Louis in support. 'He did take them prisoner and made them walk back. Then the red mist came down when he learned about Edwards.'

'Yeah, and I'm not going to lose any sleep over a few Jerries or Eyeties,' added O'Hara. 'We can't be getting all honourable about things. This is a shitshow and the pretence about things sometimes gets me confused. This whole thing is a very dirty and messy business. There is nothing straightforward or honourable about killing one another. Not many lads on either side get to die quickly or cleanly. Look what happened today with our troop and the Firefly. Most of those men did not die quickly.'

'Impett did,' muttered McGrew. 'He knew nothing about it at all.'

'What happened?' asked Wingnut nervously.

'He was unloading a truck full of supplies when an air attack happened,' McGrew answered. 'The lorry was full of ammunition and Impett was on the back unloading when the Jerry aircraft strafed the area. It shot over and gave a passing blast. The lorry was blown from here to kingdom come and our Impett went with it.'

'All the way to the promised land,' muttered Louis.

'Bloody hell,' said Wingnut, clearly shocked.

'It was the day after he got his Panzer IV,' said McGrew.

'You have to be careful when you achieve something in the troop. You get a result and then good old Lady Luck comes along and sticks her arse in your face and farts,' said Meadows.

'Lady Luck has got a shit sense of humour,' agreed McGrew.

Meadows finally took a cigarette and offered the pack about. Each man graciously accepted. The dismal candlelight lent a strange, homely glow and the chill night was abated within the cramped confines of the tank by the smell of petrol, body odour and a faint lingering of cordite.

It was against all protocol. Everything in the manual and all they had been taught was forgotten – a foolish and neglectful thing that would have got them into serious trouble had Squadron HQ had any inkling. But after the crew finished their smoking they then gradually fell asleep one by one. Including Sergeant McGrew.

CHAPTER 12

IN THE MORNING MIST

'Jesus Christ!' exclaimed McGrew.

'What?' Meadows woke with a start.

'We've all fallen asleep!' he answered as he stood up and made for his periscope.

'What's gone wrong,' groaned O'Hara in the background.

Both the candles were still burning but they were close to the wick. Louis and Wingnut began to stir too. Gradually, the Cromwell tank's crewmen woke from their slumber. Louis opened his driver's hatch and O'Hara opened his. Meadows stood up to open the loader's hatch.

'It's full of mist outside but the morning light is well and truly out there. It must be around seven if it's light.'

One by one, each trooper climbed out and dismounted from the tank. Each man wanting to stretch his legs.

'This is not good,' muttered Louis. 'Squadron HQ will go blooming mad if they find out we all fell asleep.'

'I don't think Serge will tell them, aye, Serge?' O'Hara commented sarcastically.

McGrew was equally dry with his reply, 'Well, I'm the commander of this unit. So, I'm of the opinion to let me and the rest of you off with a stern warning.'

'That works for me, Serge,' said Meadows.

'Oh, aye, me too,' O'Hara answered.

'I'll not call in yet,' said McGrew. 'Who's going to get a brew going?'

'I'll do it,' said Meadows as he clambered back up. He had stretched his legs enough.

McGrew whispered, 'Throw us down the toilet paper. I want to see a man about a dog.'

Meadows went to the Jerry box. It was newly strapped down among the replaced stowage. He lifted the flap and threw a toilet roll to the sergeant.

'Enjoy, Serge,' he said, smiling.

'I'll try to,' replied McGrew snootily.

'Yer not going to do it under here are you, Serge?' O'Hara's black-ringed eyes looked concerned.

'I'll pop outside around the bush. I'll find somewhere quiet in the morning mist,' he replied.

'Do you want me to keep watch...' Wingnut trailed off, realising his offer was inappropriate.

'I don't think that will be necessary, lad.' McGrew quietly sauntered off out of the front entrance.

'I think I'll need to go when he comes back,' said Louis.

'Me too,' added Wingnut. 'We'll have to take turns.'

'Better than inside the tank in an ammo box,' said O'Hara.

'Have you ever had to do that?' asked Wingnut.

'Yeah, lots of times,' O'Hara replied.

'Meadows is the worst,' added Louis. 'He ruddy stinks.'

'Yeah, we'll encourage him to go outside and squeeze one out before we go back.'

There was an eerie silence within the morning mist, a peculiarity that was unsettling. McGrew breathed out his warm vapour as he walked around the huge bush and found a recess in the holly. The sergeant looked all about him – nothing much beyond twenty to maybe thirty feet. The morning mist was heavy. It would probably clear as the day moved on.

McGrew undid his pixie suit and shivered in the cold morning air as he squatted with his bare bottom close to a gap in the holly. There he remained, contentedly looking directly through the mist towards the ghostly forms of broken trees of the wood opposite. A few silver birches had survived the previous night's bombardment. The place where he, Louis and Wingnut had left three dead German soldiers. The mist was becoming patchy but remained thick in parts. He could only catch glimpses of tree trunk through small wispy gaps. And so, while about his function of convenience, he contented himself with such challenging visual exploits. His eyes wandered, exploring every faint gap in the morning mist. Then he abruptly stopped at one such gap. His vision settled upon something coarse and faintly white. A dismal white with ghosting streaks of green and yellow grinning through the thin, watery white overlay. McGrew blinked and had to look again. Were his eyes playing tricks on him? He reaffirmed that his vision was not impaired in any way. He was staring at metal. Then he saw the insignia of a black cross on a white background. The vision hit him like a slap in the face. How on earth did such a vehicle manage to get to that place without being spotted or heard?

His heart skipped a beat and a wave of fright pushed down in his stomach. Any thought of constipation was redundant as his release was instant, a cascade of stools erupting down into the bush.

'Oh my God!' he cursed quietly to himself. 'More blooming déjà vu. Ruddy North Africa all over again.'

McGrew quickly and nervously tore off some toilet paper as he tried to think what he needed to do. The slope of the metal had *Zimmerit* covering it, the camouflage grinning through the coarse whitewash. The mist parted a little more as he caught sight of the tracks. It was the chassis of a Panzer III. But it wasn't the tank. It was the Sturmgeschütz III, an assault gun on tracks. Its gun overlooked the approach road on the other side of the river. It was preparing the usual type of trap.

'Oh, my word,' he muttered under his breath. 'Wingnut had guessed it correctly. And right under our Tommy noses. Right under every Tommy nose. Jerry has sent a big gun up the incline when the bombardment was happening. It is now hidden within the smashed trees with a grand overlook. A few shots and then off down the narrow embankment. Hit and run, hit and run. Oh, you sneaky devious Jerry sods.'

McGrew quickly finished his business. He was growing in confidence and realised that the entire side of the Sturmgeschütz was exposed to Molly's gun. She had a clear view of the enemy assault vehicle. Inadvertently, the Jerry assault gun on tracks had placed herself smack bang in front of Molly's spiteful little gun barrel. A barrel hidden within a huge holly bush. At such a range, their Cromwell tank couldn't miss. At that minor distance, his tank crew could take their pick of any vulnerable area. Sergeant McGrew could barely contain his excitement. The enemy assault gun was oblivious to Molly and her crew.

Quickly, he crept back and entered the confines of the tank's hideout. 'I need the toilet paper, Serge,' said Louis.

'No bleeding chance,' he hissed back excitedly and put his finger over his lips for hush.

Louis looked confused and whispered, 'What's wrong.'

'What's wrong? I'll tell you what's right, Louis.' McGrew's harsh Belfast accent was radiant with delight – wicked and spiteful pleasure.

'That must have been one hell of a clear out,' muttered Meadows.

'Everyone mount up inside Molly now, and quietly. No noise – as quiet as possible,' McGrew hissed.

Once again, they clambered inside the tank. The sergeant's need for urgency and stealth was not lost on any of them. Everyone settled inside before he continued.

'Alright now, lads, I want you all to turn your periscopes to that wood we went to last night. The very woodland our lads hit in the bombardment.'

'What are we looking for, Serge?' asked O'Hara.

'Keep looking, Billy boy! You'll see a real big-breasted tart. A rather naughty-looking one. A dirty all-night stop-out. The sexy type of bitch that doesn't know when to go home. The sort you see in the early hours still propping up the bar. She's been there all night until the early hours of this morning. Right under our noses. No one heard her and no one saw her enter the establishment when the party was in full swing. And she's not looking at the dance floor anymore – it's empty. Or so she thinks. The lady doesn't know we're here, eyeing her up from our little obscure alcove.'

Meadows looked aghast. 'This happened the last time you went off for a sneaky one, Serge. When you were in the desert getting your tooth done. Almost déjà vu follows you like a ruddy lovesick puppy.'

The troopers' periscopes could see through the gaps in the bush but they were straining for a moment as each could only see mist. Then Louis was the first to hiss in surprise. 'Jesus Christ! That is one dirty old stop-out. A Sturmgeschütz with all her wears. Blimey, all up close and flaunting it.'

Then the rest looked more intently, their interest tickled as each trooper saw the beast of a machine before Molly's gun barrel.

'Bloody hell,' hissed Meadows. 'She's a big old bird. What a gorgeous tart she would make. There you go, Wingnut, that's what a real "mess you up" girl looks like. Do you think this brass is too much tart for you to handle? Or are you going to let this seasoned bitch put some hairs on your chest?'

'Blimey, that's a bit out of my league on the naughty lady front. A real big Sturmgeschütz up close and bending over,' said Wingnut excitedly, taking up the naughty lads' banter with utter glee. 'Is she a mark three or a four?'

'It's a Panzer III chassis,' replied O'Hara. 'Not as many fours about, so I'm told. These tarts usually come as threes, that's for sure.'

'That's right,' replied Meadows, 'waiting for a bunch of hairy-arsed blokes like us to come along and touch her up. Are we going to pump a few into her? The blooming naughty bitch.'

'Alright now, lads, we'll give this old gal one, good and proper,' added McGrew excitedly. 'Meadows, load one up and Wingnut, I want to select spots under the wheel vendors – below the top track and support rollers into the side armour. There are two armour skirts covering the wheels and tracks to the front. They stop just short to expose the front sprocket, so the shot is viable. And can you see where the last panel ends near the middle of the chassis? There we have a nice convenient gap because the protective skirt plate is gone. Two of them are missing, in fact.'

'I got that, Serge,' said Wingnut, bubbling with enthusiasm. 'Bloody hell, we've really caught this Jerry with her drawers down.'

'I agree, we've caught Jerry good and proper,' added Meadows good-humouredly. He started to whisper the loading drill protocol as he slid a selected shell into the breech. It was followed by a customary slap on Wingnut's leg. The recruit was ready with the gun and waiting for McGrew's further instructions.

'The height of decadence,' said Louis chuckling, unable to resist Wingnut's comical remark.

McGrew grinned at the camaraderie and continued to instruct his method of attack. 'We'll put the first shot into the sprocket wheel up front. Jerry likes his sprockets to the front. Then, to finish, we'll hit again with two more shots midway into the side armour below the upper track and the upper support rollers. The plating is thinner and more vulnerable there. But the first shot must count. We need to smash that front sprocket. If the track sprocket is out then our Jerry can't do much. We'll have time to be more precise with the killing shots. The Sturmgeschütz has no turret and therefore the whole vehicle has to turn to get a shot back at us. That can't happen if we've taken out a sprocket wheel. We're going to hit the bitch fast and quick. A crippling shot and then a help yourself and pick off the juicy parts shot. We'll teach the sneaky sods to try and get one over on us, that's for sure.'

'What if it rotates the other way on its other tracks?' asked O'Hara.

There followed a silent pause before Louis replied, 'It will be a right struggle and the Jerry crew might not work that out quick enough with the first impact shot.'

'No one loves a smart-arse, Billy,' added McGrew jokingly.

Meadows tapped Wingnut on the leg again to signify the breech was loaded.

McGrew held his finger up and whispered, 'Not just yet, Wingnut, wait for my command. Meadows, stand ready to quicky load a second and then a third.

'Billy, I'll be wanting you to shoot any jumping Jerry coming out of that machine, now. No messing about – show them who's the man, d'ya hear me, Billy "boy" O'Hara?'

'I got yer, Serge. I'm ready, that's for sure.'

'Right then. Wingnut, focus on that front sprocket now, lad. Just before the metal skirt covers.'

'I'm bang on the money, Serge,' Wingnut whispered. A line of sweat ran down and around his eye socket. He took no notice of it and stood waiting for the order.

McGrew said, 'Five, four, three, two, one, fire!'

Wingnut fired and the breech kicked back as McGrew called, 'Reload!'

The Sturmgeschütz's sprocket was torn apart as the impact smashed the wheel. The clang of ruptured iron and the eruption of metal fragments threw steel splinters out of the expanding smoke. A distant bell-like echoing lingered for a second or two.

'Reload!' shouted McGrew.

Meadows was now shouting out his loading drill instruction after quickly removing the spent shell casing. He finished by slamming the second shell into the breech and locking it before slapping the gunner's leg once again.

Sure of the initial damage to the Sturmgeschütz, Wingnut had moved his gunsight to the middle section of the enemy vehicle – just below the top track and at the thinner armoured plate. Confident of the sighting, he squeezed the trigger and let loose the second shell. All watched as Molly's speeding missile smacked an all-pervading hole into the side armour below the small upper tracks and rollers. Smoke appeared about the strike, quickly obscuring the hit.

Instantly, Meadows released the spent shell casing again, screaming out his regulatory protocol while loading a third shot and locking the breech mechanism.

Wingnut received the tap on the leg and fired his third shot close to his second hit. Another strike as more smoke exploded from the speeding projectile's wicked impact. This time there was the unmistakeable quick glow like a flickering light within the seams of the hatches and cupola. The original hole from the central strike glowed now too.

'Reload!'

Wingnut received a fourth tap on the leg as he fixed the gunsight for a fourth shot.

McGrew called out, 'Hold fire there, Wingnut. The next one is to go up the birdie's fat arse.'

'Here they come!' shouted O'Hara with wicked triumph.

Just below the long barrel of the Sturmgeschütz, a lower front hatch opened. An enemy trooper's upper half emerged.

O'Hara was on the figure like a whippet. His Besa sang out with a short burst of four shots. The man twisted as he was hit. Fine red-speckled wisps sprayed behind as the bullets ripped through the unfortunate enemy trooper. He fell back down into the hatch.

The cupola opened and as the commander emerged, O'Hara's machine gun fired off another quick four-shot burst. The enemy commander's arms clutched and his head jerked back as a draught of blood erupted from his skull. He toppled back and fell behind the blind side of the Sturmgeschütz.

'Two have escaped from the blind side, Serge,' called Louis.

'Start her up, Louis,' shouted McGrew, his adrenalin running.

Wingnut received another tap on the leg and he called out, 'Fourth round ready, Serge. Tell us when?'

McGrew screamed excitedly as Molly roared into life – the sergeant's adrenalin was running at full pace. 'Will do, Wingnut. Hold fire there, lad. I'll tell you when. Take us around the back of the slag, Louis. We're putting one in the old cow's arse.' He looked to O'Hara. 'Billy, if the two that got out are going to surrender, let them. Take them prisoner if possible.'

'Aye, Serge,' he replied.

Molly rose and erupted out of the giant holly bush like a monstrous forest banshee emerging from her lair. The long tree trunk still lay across her front with clumps of thick bracken disguising her threatening appearance. Before them was the burning and smoking Sturmgeschütz – the action was still playing out.

'A fine kill, Wingnut,' McGrew said as he put on his headphones and went up to open the cupola to help get rid of the acrid cordite smell. Meadows and Louis did the same thing with their hatches. The smell of cordite was almost nauseating within a few seconds of action.

McGrew gulped in the cold morning air and looked out through the damp mist. Before them was the burning Sturmgeschütz. The sergeant felt a swell of gratification as Louis steered Molly around the burning and smoking wreck. The turret's gun swung around to aim at the rear of the mounted artillery vehicle. He called into the microphone.

'Wingnut, have you got the lady in sight?'

'I have, Serge,' he answered enthusiastically.

'Three, two, one, fire!'

Wingnut put the fourth shell into the back at point-blank range. As more fire erupted and smoke billowed up, McGrew could make out two frightened enemy crewmen standing aside within the trees. Each trooper had his hands raised in surrender.

Again, McGrew spoke through his microphone, 'I have two prisoners, don't shoot. They have raised hands.'

The sergeant pulled out his revolver and pointed it at the two surviving enemy crewmen of the wrecked Sturmgeschütz. 'Come forward!'

Cautiously, the two anxious men walked towards the Cromwell tank with their hands raised. They were dressed in baggy, padded grey winter clothing with an outer belt around their middle. One was wearing a quilt-lined hat – thermal insulation with a detachable chin and mouth guard. The other wore what looked like a Russian ushanka-style hat. Each man must have been fighting in extreme weather conditions, perhaps from the Eastern Front. The prisoners did not look the way McGrew would expect the average Panzer troopers to dress. They seemed rather scruffy.

'Are there any more of these Sturmgeschütz up here?'

'No,' replied one of the troopers. 'We are the only unit.'

It was feasible but the trooper would hardly inform on any others. McGrew stared down suspiciously and tried to gauge the man's expression. He knew the enemy trooper was frightened. That much was obvious.

'Walk in front of the tank and keep your hands raised. Do you understand?'

'Yes,' replied the man who then spoke in German to his friend, translating McGrew's words.

McGrew switched his microphone to the A setting and called over the net to his Troop Command post, instructing them that his unit had taken the Sturmgeschütz lying in wait to attack traffic on the approach road across the river. He asked for permission to return to base with his prisoners. His request was granted.

He noticed the mist was clearing as he switched to the B setting and instructed all over the intercom.

'Alright, lads, we're clear to return and we must stick and move along the side of the steep precipice going down to the river. Advance upwards with caution. Our lads know we're coming in. How's things for you, Louis?'

'Alright, Serge. The mist is clearing rapidly and I can see across the river now.'

McGrew smiled. 'How about you, Billy?'

'Aye,' he replied. 'I've got both prisoners covered in front.'

'Wingnut,' began McGrew, 'good shooting, lad. And Meadows, great loading. A good kill. A bloody good kill. Well done.'

At the same moment, a barrage of artillery guns roared into life and once again, Allied shells whistled over and down into the already smashed and bombed basin.

'Here we go again,' muttered Louis as he steered Molly.

Scattered platoons of tanks emerged from the woods. Some were Cromwell tanks with Sherman Fireflys accompanying them. There were also platoons of Sherman and Churchill tanks. Infantry and other motorised vehicles moved behind the advancing tank formations under cover of the bombardment.

Across the river, more Allied formations moved along the clear road. The very place the burning Sturmgeschütz was waiting to attack.

'Blimey,' said Louis. 'This is a full-on advance. It must be happening right along the lines.'

McGrew spoke into his intercom, 'These Jerries wouldn't have been able to do much, even if she had fired a few shots off. Look at this lot. One Sturmgeschütz was certainly biting off more than she could chew.'

'Well, I hope the lads across the river will show us some appreciation, especially the lot at the front of the line.' Meadows chuckled.

'That's for sure,' shouted O'Hara, keeping his machine gun upon the German prisoners walking ahead of the tank. 'They would have been plum targets.'

'This time we get to pass our lads advancing to the fight while we go to the back of the line and safety,' said Meadows.

'You're not going to do your George Formby bit, are you?' asked Louis, giggling.

'Oh no, don't load the bloke's rifle,' said O'Hara, laughing.

Meadows grinned. 'Oh, what do you mean?' And then he did his bad George Formby impersonation with an unimpressive Lancashire accent: 'It's turned out nice again.'

'Stop Molly, Louis!' The sudden instruction came over the intercom. The driver complied and all heard Sergeant McGrew calling to the prisoners.

'Hey, Jerry!'

O'Hara and Louis watched the two prisoners stop and slowly turn to face the tank. They seemed confused and frightened.

'What's going on?' asked Wingnut.

Even over the rumbling neutral engine, O'Hara could make out the conversation. 'Did you not understand that radio banter? The top brass seems to think the prisoners were lying about other enemy units. But the prisoners are insisting there are none. They're insisting their Sturmgeschütz is the only one. I think the sergeant has had report of a second.'

'That seems unlikely up here,' added Louis.

McGrew dropped down from the cupola. 'Louis, Billy, get up through your hatches and push that camouflage shit off the front of Molly. I think we almost got fired upon by our own side – our lads across the river – at this distance, their spotters mistook us for a hostile. Get the camouflaging stuff off our front as quick as—'

Suddenly, an instantaneous ear-splitting bang shook Molly – steel against steel. A shattering, tremendous clang. Inside, each man shook violently and went deaf amid erupting smoke and wickedly hot, glowing spall spinning through the confines of their Molly mare. Screams and cusses were smothered by choking smoke. The whole tank violently wobbled as each man convulsed at the dreadful impact. McGrew had smashed against the water tanks and the tool box. He thought his teeth would shake from his gums. The rising acrid smoke obscured everything about him. He had heard the two lumps of spall hit the radio close to him. There were screams as the searing heat spread within the smoke-filled turret. He distinctly heard Wingnut's agonised roar during the confusion of smoke and intense heat. He could remember the convulsive coughing as he slid down onto the turret's floor and the blackness taking him.

McGrew came to and felt helping hands grab him. He was being lifted up onto his feet in the darkness and the choking smoke. The screams of confusion came from within and outside the tank. Hands were reaching down through the cupola to his instinctively upraised wrists. Then he remembered someone wrapping their arms about his shins and bodily hoisting him upwards to the cupola hatch. Helpful arms were behind him and hooked under his armpits, dragging him out and off the burning turret. He managed to gulp in the cold winter air and made out the voices of Louis and O'Hara along with the German prisoners. The *Panzergrenadiers* had helped rescue his two crewmen at the front of Molly – they'd been pulled out of the burning wreckage via their front exit hatches. Louis and the two German troopers were trying to persuade O'Hara not to go back into the burning tank. Then a second strike slammed into the front of the already burning Molly. They shook violently under the second impact. Flame erupted from the front of the vehicle as the plucky little tank burned. Dazed and fighting to remain conscious, McGrew vaguely realised Molly was in her death throes. Their loveable little mare was finished. He was being dragged off the flaming wreck.

'It's all over bar the shouting,' he cussed and passed out for a second time.

McGrew regained consciousness again, moments later. His feet were at ten to two and he stared down through his splayed boots. They were being dragged along – the heels scraping over the frozen soil. Firm hands were under his armpits, pulling him away as a plume of fire erupted upwards from Molly – the inferno that their burning tank had become. Then McGrew heard the screams! Hoarse, agonising shrieks! Dire squeals of insufferable agony as the wretched trapped inside Molly's burning armour was roasted alive. A second ball of orange inferno erupted, expanding out and engulfing Molly again, flames wickedly raging about the tank. The wretched trooper's screams were gone. A haunting déjà vu echoed in McGrew's memory.

The distraught sergeant watched the faithful steel steed in her burning death throes. 'Thank God those agonised screams have stopped,' he whispered to himself.

McGrew felt his rescuer come to a stop. His feet remained at ten to two as he began to sob.

O'Hara was still trying to fight with Louis and the German *Panzergrenadiers*. He wanted to go back but was being physically and robustly restrained amid shouts of earnest protest.

'Déjà vu! Déjà vu!' groaned McGrew. 'Oh my God, Wingnut! Oh God, it's all over now. Not again. You said Wingnut had the look of a poor sod, Meadows.

'Oh my God!' McGrew gulped as he tried to contain the tears. 'More wicked déjà vu. Will this bloody shitshow never let up, now? You always said he wouldn't make it, Meadows. I was hoping, just for once, you might be wrong. But you got it right again. Do you not get fed up with always being so blooming right, Meadows? This is the fourth time you've pulled me out of one of them burning bastards. Next time, leave me in there. This is getting too much.'

The Allied tanks, and all other manner of mechanised vehicles, continued to slowly advance under the umbrella of bombardment. Infantry units were huddled behind the multitude of tanks. The advance towards the Reichswald forest area was beginning. A Red Cross lorry rumbled down the scarp towards them as a firm, placating hand rested upon his shoulder.

'Sorry, Serge. I'm so sorry. We couldn't get the poor sod out!' It was a sympathetic cockney accent. The voice of Wingnut.

'Wingnut?' gasped McGrew, shocked. 'Oh my God!' He looked back at the burning tank. 'Oh my God, Meadows. What did you do, Meadows? He saved me as the second shell struck. He got me out.'

'I'm so sorry, Serge. I'm really sorry. But there was nothing we could do for him once that second shell hit Molly,' continued Wingnut compassionately.

McGrew snorted and tried to hold back the remorse. He bent his head back to look into the grey morning sky and opened his mouth. No sound came out, and he didn't notice that the morning mist was completely gone. Just thick black smoke coupled with the smell of cordite and death. He screwed his tear-soaked eyes shut and then gritted his teeth. If he tried hard enough, he might be able to will his person back to that kind and blessed memory. That little alcove in eternity. He imagined himself as a bird flying over the desert sands towards a rumbling Bedford truck moving across a dusty track in North Africa. He dived down and entered through the rear opening of the truck's flap where he could sit among his fellow tank crewmen, when they had all been happy for a day. He saw Caterpillar Miller, Nuts and Bolts, Impett, Harry Edwards and his four-time rescuer, John Meadows. They were all sitting in the truck as it bounced over the sandy terrain.

All of them holding up a bottle of beer and smiling at him. He noted Meadows lightly wiggling a fine bottle of Irish whiskey before him. He was smiling and winked once. Then all the lads began to sing in a perfect harmony of well-tuned voices.

With his eyes shut tight, McGrew began to sing with them, pitifully moving with gut-wrenching remorse...

Oh! I eat watermelon and I have for years,
sing Polly-wolly-doodle all the day;
I like watermelon but it wets my ears,
sing Polly-wolly-doodle all the day.

Maybe grass tastes good to a moo cow's mouth,
sing Polly-wolly-doodle all the day;
But I like chicken 'cause I'm from the south,
sing Polly-wolly-doodle all the day.

Fare-thee well,
Fare-thee well,
Mister gloom be on your way.

The tank continued to burn. O'Hara had stopped struggling against Louis and the German prisoners. Moments ago, they were trying to kill one another and then they were trying to save each other. After accepting the cost had been too high, they did the bittersweet thing. Louis passed around his cigarettes and the two German prisoners accepted with sad gratitude.

'Déjà vu,' muttered O'Hara.

'I think we are all back in the desert again,' replied Louis sadly.

'This is déjà vu with those Eyeties again. But the sergeant is back in the lorry, the day before. He always goes back there,' said O'Hara sadly.

'Singing Polly-wolly-doodle all the day,' replied Louis with his swelling eyes, the forewarning of an oozing cascade. Tears brimmed in his swollen eyes and gently rolled down his dark brown cheeks, falling from his jaw to the uncaring soil. A ground that contained everything. An earth that would take every tiny teardrop splattering upon its cold, hard surface. The callous, unfeeling sod that would nonchalantly absorb all the heartbreak of the world.

The ambulance came to a halt as Sergeant McGrew sat there with his legs outstretched. He was still singing his nostalgic song. Wingnut watched over the sad sight of his momentarily broken sergeant. The bloodied recruit understood why the song had sad memories for McGrew. An invented déjà vu. A searched-for reminiscence that was not to be indulged lightly.

AUTHOR'S NOTE

During the year 1979, at the age of eighteen, I got a job at the General Post Office based at the King Edward Building. This was one of London's many postal sorting offices. The GPO ended shortly afterwards, and it became known as the Royal Mail.

At this time, the King Edward Building accommodated the Eastern Central Delivery office, and the Foreign Section offices upstairs. I worked in the FS, after a brief spell downstairs at the ECDO.

Today, in 2021, I am sixty years of age. Back in 1979, many of the men that were of this age were war veterans, especially in the Post Office where I remained for almost twenty years. I left at the end of 1998 after all the war veterans had retired. Most of these larger-than-life characters are now gone – if any are still alive, they would be in their late nineties or over one hundred years of age. When I think back to these men, it does sometimes bring a lump to my throat. I can still see them laughing and joking about us youngsters not having any idea of what comes along in life. Some were humorous and some were rather grumpy. But they were all men of some merit.

The King Edward Building could boast an ex-serviceman from every single theatre of the war – the Army, the Royal Navy and the RAF, including Fighter, Bomber and Coastal Command, and the Royal Navy's Fleet Air Arm.

There were hundreds of ex-war veterans working throughout the building and I spoke to a great many of them as a young man. I remember one postman teaching me the delivery round of Upper Thames Street in London's EC4 district. It was enjoyable and all the deliveries were along the River Thames. This man's name was George Saunders and he was only fifty-four in 1979. We used to go to a small café in Paternoster Square near St Paul's Cathedral after the morning delivery. We would have a cup of coffee and a smoke – talk about the world and all its problems. I remember George telling me that he was a rear gunner in the bombers flying over Germany. He was in the RAF from 1943 to 1945. He also told me that many of his friends never survived the war.

Another man was called Frankie Dearman. He was captured in the Desert War and spent much time as a POW in Italy where he liked the people. He was also held in Germany, where he was not so keen. Frank told me the guards were fine, but Italy's environment was preferable.

There was also another ex-Desert Rat who knew me because he worked with my grandfather's brother, my uncle, Tom Powell. He left the FS about two weeks before I joined from the ECDO downstairs. I think he must have told Joe about me before I went upstairs into the FS. To my surprise Joe knew about me – he had a daughter who lived next door to my parents in Hornchurch, Essex. Joe was a smartly dressed black man with glasses. I always remember him wearing long grey dust jackets and beneath the attire, he always wore a collar and tie. I also remember he had a rusty voice, as though he spoke from the back of his throat. Joe and other 8th Army men told odd stories of their time during the desert campaign. Some recollections were humorous and some were dark and dreadful.

These men would have numbered in their hundreds throughout the entire King Edward Building, where around three thousand postal workers were employed over various shifts. Early shifts, day shifts, late and night shifts kept the sorting office going every day of the year. The KEB was a place where many of these war veterans saw out their pre-retirement years. I often see a face, in my mind's eye, someone telling me of their past. Then I have to remind myself that the old veteran is probably no longer with us. There was a very small man of about five feet two, by my estimation. He was having a retirement day. I was holding the fort from his sorting frame of the South America road while many people came back and forth to wish him a happy retirement. In the Post Office, at that time, the retirement age was sixty, but one could stay on for five extra years if one wanted to. This small man decided to leave at sixty-four. On his final day, in 1980, he was telling me he had been in the Post Office since 1931, from the age of fifteen. He said he had an interval of absence during the war when he was conscripted into the Army. He was at Normandy in 1944, but it was several days after the landing when the area was secured. He also mentioned that he remembered the Crystal Palace fire in 1936. I can't remember what the man's name was and I never saw him again after that day. There were people like this all over the place. Now they're all gone – all of those veterans gradually retiring one by one.

Some things in this story are inspired by their tales. Fables that are twisted and re-invented into different parables for this fictional novel. It is with kind memories of these many veterans that I would like to dedicate this fictional war story.

Printed in Great Britain
by Amazon